The DEEP TIME Diaries

as Recorded by
Neesha and Jon Olifee

and

Transcribed by Gary Raham

To Kate —
Enjoy the journey!
Gary Raham

fulcrum resources
Golden, Colorado

This book is dedicated to Hilda, for nourishing a sense of wonder. And to Roy,
for demanding dedication to a task.

Many thanks to Suzanne Barchers, who, while editor at Fulcrum Publishing, not only recognized
potential in *The Deep Time Diaries*, but provided the suggestions to give it the right focus and
voice. Thanks as well to Fulcrum editor Susan Hill, who nurtured the book to completion; to
Patty Maher, for her design and production expertise; and to Jill Scott, for singing its praises.
Dick Scott and Jason Cook provided invaluable help with their reviews and edits.

Special thanks to my northern Colorado writers' brain trust that included: Laura Backes,
Carol Crowley, Beverly Haley, Ellen Howard, Sean McCollum, Nancy Phillips, Clare Rutherford,
and Linda White. Their suggestions and encouragement helped me create form from a chaos of
raw ideas at the expense of learning more about dinosaurs than they ever cared to know.

May my wife, Sharon, forgive me for a house full of books and fossils, and may Deanna and
Lindsay survive their exploitation as models and rough draft readers. They all support and
inspire me in countless ways.

Library of Congress Cataloging-in-Publication Data
Raham, Gary.
   The deep time diaries : as recorded by Neesha and Jon Olifee / and transcribed by Gary
Raham.
      p. cm.
Summary: The fictional diaries of a family from the twenty-second century that discovers
a time machine which takes them back through Earth's ancient past. Includes related
activities, maps, bibliographies, and glossary.
   ISBN 1-55591-415-2 (pbk.)
   [1. Time travel—Fiction. 2. Diaries—Fiction. 3. Science
fiction.] I. Title.
   PZ7.R12719 Dg 2000
   [Fic]—dc21
00-010126

Printed in China

0 9 8 7 6 5 4 3 2 1

Fulcrum Publishing
16100 Table Mountain Parkway, Suite 300
Golden, Colorado 80403
(800) 992-2908 • (303) 277-1623
www.fulcrum-resources.com

Contents

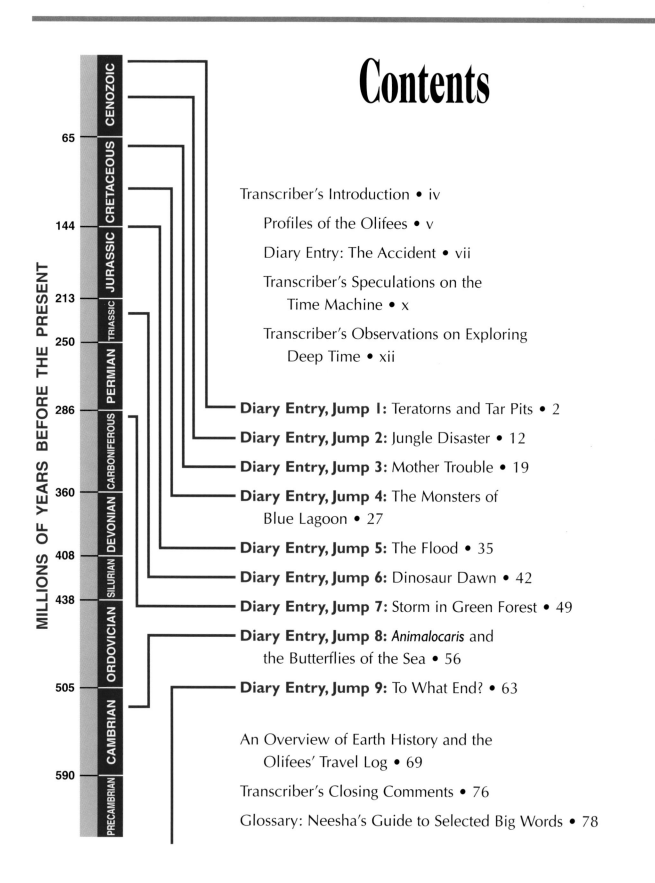

Transcriber's Introduction

Three facts summarize what scientists know about the discovery of what have come to be called *The Deep Time Diaries:*

- Two paleontologists, while searching for Precambrian fossils (more than 500 million years old), discovered complex artifacts—capsules made of unknown metal-polymer alloys—embedded in ancient rocks of the MacDonnell Ranges, west of Alice Springs in the Northern Territory of Australia.
- One capsule (with its encrypted vacuum seal intact) contained drawings and text, written in English, that describe an incredible story of travel and adventure in Earth's distant past.
- Radiometric dating confirmed the age of the capsule's contents and the surrounding rock to be 800 million years old—far older than complex life on Earth.

Until now, only a small group of scientists and world leaders have had access to the contents of these diaries and drawings, believed to have been created by a human family who originated in our future—perhaps the early–22nd century. This book serves to share a large portion of the Diaries with the world in the hope that others can shed light on exactly who Miriam, Gregory, Neesha, and Jon Olifee were (or will be) and who (or what) created the time shuttle they used to witness the dramatic, prehistoric events you will soon read about. Contemporary maps show the present-day locations of the Olifees' adventures for those who wish to trace their journey more closely and explore the fossil remains of the amazing creatures that preceded us on Planet Earth.

Profiles of the Olifees

The Diaries represent Jon and Neesha's personal records. Scientists are still searching for official trip logs, but fear that time and the elements may have destroyed them. Miriam Olifee was apparently a professional paleontologist. Greg, her husband, studied exobiology and competently sketched much of what the Olifees saw on their journey. Jon was Miriam and Greg's oldest child, a boy of perhaps thirteen or so who was interested in astronomy and dinosaurs. Neesha, Jon's sister, was a year or two younger and had a fondness for bugs and chocolate (not necessarily in that order).

Here's how Neesha and Jon described each other:

Neesha about Jon:

"Jon's a Borg, but he has his *moments*. He always seems to be there when I really need him, like when I step into tar pits and dino nurseries—which has been a little too often lately. He just needs to remember he's my brother and not a grub rancher.

"Hmmm. If Jon were a vegetable I think he'd be broccoli. A broccoli stalk with contacts and hiking boots. Except broccoli doesn't make near enough noise.

"Jon's idea of a good time is to lie on a damp, sandy beach in the middle of the night and count meteors. He asked a girl to do that with him once, but all she counted was several dozen sand fleas pole-vaulting her leg hairs.

"Jon says forget all the sci-fi stuff you've read. The chance of two hi-tech civilizations being alive at the same time and place is like a gnat and a spider mite colliding at midnight in the Astrodome Sport Museum. We're lucky to have found the time machine, he says, and we *may* even get to see the Builders. I'd rather be in the Astrodome. It's only a hundred miles from home ..."

Jon about Neesha:

"Dad measured the atmospheric oxygen content the other day at 19.3 percent and figures we're in the middle Cambrian period. But Neesha's still finding enough oxygen somewhere to babble all the time, mostly about the creepy trilobites wiggling around in the tide pools.

"I know Neesha misses her friend Landra, but she's been stuck to me like a tick lately except when it's her turn for chores.

"Mom got a little sore the other day when I asked if Neesha was adopted. Dad laughed. At least he knew I was kidding.

"The little grub nearly scared my hair white digging around in that hadrosaur nest. Mamma hadrosaur came close to flattening her like a micrometeorite on a deflector shield. Neesha held on to me for a long time, even after Dad got there. Of course after she stopped trembling she wiped the snot off her nose and told me she'd had things under control and not to butt in next time.

"Tomorrow I swear she goes on a leash ..."

THE ACCIDENT

Location: Inside One of the Builders' Asteroids (Asteroid Alpha)

8/10/22: Entry by Jon Olifee

I can't believe this place. The Builders, whoever (or whatever) they were, hollowed out the insides of these two asteroids like they were as soft as cheeseballs. Each asteroid is about ten miles in diameter. They orbit around a common center of gravity. There's a whole city inside Asteroid Alpha where the military has set up space for the research teams, including Mom and Dad. You can look up and see a few wispy clouds around the singularity sphere and approach cone.[1] Beyond them, across the axis of the asteroid, the buildings make a hazy, puzzle pattern overhead. Tomorrow Colonel Fasee wants us to report to some kind of cargo bay beneath the approach cone. He thinks my folks can help identify some specimens there.

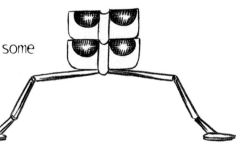

8/11/22: Entry by Jon Olifee

Mom's excited. The specimens the military found in some fancy freezer compartments haven't been alive on Earth for hundreds of millions of years. Not only that, they come from all different time periods. Mom's beginning to think the military is right about these asteroids being part of some time machine, and its builders must have been collecting Earth life for a long time ... but why?

---

[1] See the sketch of the asteroid complex (p. xi) and "Transcriber's Speculations on the Time Machine" (p. x). The singularity sphere is the physical appearance of a microscopic wormhole in the confines of the asteroid's force fields.

8/16/22: Entry by Neesha Olifee

Jon hasn't been keeping these logs very well. He's been too busy helping Mom and Dad sort stuff out. Some engineers have been poking around looking for power sources or something. One of them is kind of cute, but he can't even remember my name. "Nela, don't touch that, honey," he says, or "Nefa, I think I heard your Dad calling." So anyway, I found this neat little room nobody has bothered to look at yet. It's got places to sit and write and enough glowing panels to see by. I'm going to make my log entries now.

8/17/22: Entry by Neesha Olifee

I've pinned a lot of bugs in my day, but nothing like this! I saw this thing scooting along the wall and wondered how a beetle could ever crawl through quarantine. When I looked closer, I saw it wasn't a real bug, but some eight-legged, shiny, gray robot thing. It crawled over to a control panel and hunkered down into a small depression next to a row of touch pads. With its legs pulled in, it became just another touch pad on the panel. I waited and watched two more "bugs" do the same thing. I have to tell Mom and Dad about this!

8/18/22: Entry by Neesha Olifee

So much for neat little places nobody knows anything about. Dad, Mom, Jon, and that cute engineer are all in here poking around. The "bugs" filled up the depressions on the panel and won't budge when you pull on them. Gotta go. Something's up.

Time is just one darn thing
after another.
—Neesha

8/18/22, 1800 hours: Rushed entry by Jon Olifee

My sister, the grub, has managed to find trouble again. I'm with her and Mom and Dad inside this "room" where she has been hiding out, which turns out to be some kind of shuttle. When an indicator light inside the shuttle started flashing, Dr. Crenshaw went outside to check the power panel he was working with yesterday. The door sealed behind him and won't open. The shuttle is ... [illegible] ... and I can feel us moving. Wow! One whole section of our shuttle wall just turned transparent! We're moving across the "cargo bay" area, or whatever it is, to a spot beneath the approach cone. Colonel Fasee is out there yelling at ... [illegible] ... is running all around. The shuttle is rising now and the nose is pointing toward the wormhole. The bugs Neesha was talking about ... [illegible] ... assembling themselves into something bigger ... kind of like a flying wastebasket with arms. It's babbling at us, pointing toward padded chairs rising up through spaces on the floor. We're all sitting down now and the shuttle is rumbling. It's going to launch—toward the shifting, rainbow like surface of the wormhole! ... [illegible] ... beautiful and scary. The cargo bay is dropping away behind us. Mom and Dad are yelling at each other, Neesha is crying. I can't ... [short, illegible section at end of entry].

The distinction between past, present and the future is only an illusion, even if a stubborn one.
—Albert Einstein

Is Einstein's theory a crazy vagary?
It surely is.
—The New York Times
1921

What seest thou else in the dark backward abysm of time?
—William Shakespeare

And the end and the beginning were always there.
Before the beginning and after the end.
And all is always now.
—T. S. Eliot

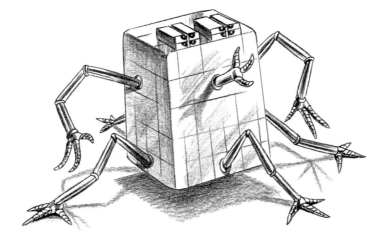

TRANSCRIBER'S SPECULATIONS ON THE TIME MACHINE

Scientists believe the time machine described by the Olifees was created by some unknown race well over 800 million years ago. No one knows why they built it near Earth or why they would have abandoned it. The term "time machine" is really too simple to describe what these ancient beings created.

They hollowed out two large asteroids and somehow suspended a speck of superdense matter called a mini–black hole at the center of each of them. The intense gravity of these mini–black holes poked openings called wormholes in the very fabric of space-time in our universe. Like a worm boring through an apple, the shuttle, also of alien design and technology, was able to bore through time by passing through one of the wormholes. It then reappeared through the other wormhole at some point in the distant past. Each time a traveler looped through the wormholes, he or she jumped farther and farther back in time.

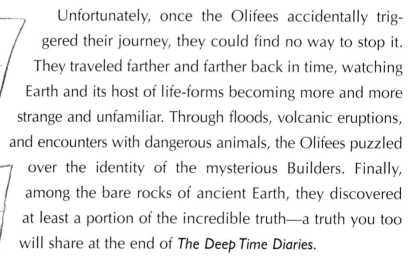

Unfortunately, once the Olifees accidentally triggered their journey, they could find no way to stop it. They traveled farther and farther back in time, watching Earth and its host of life-forms becoming more and more strange and unfamiliar. Through floods, volcanic eruptions, and encounters with dangerous animals, the Olifees puzzled over the identity of the mysterious Builders. Finally, among the bare rocks of ancient Earth, they discovered at least a portion of the incredible truth—a truth you too will share at the end of *The Deep Time Diaries*.

Asteroid/Time Machine Complex

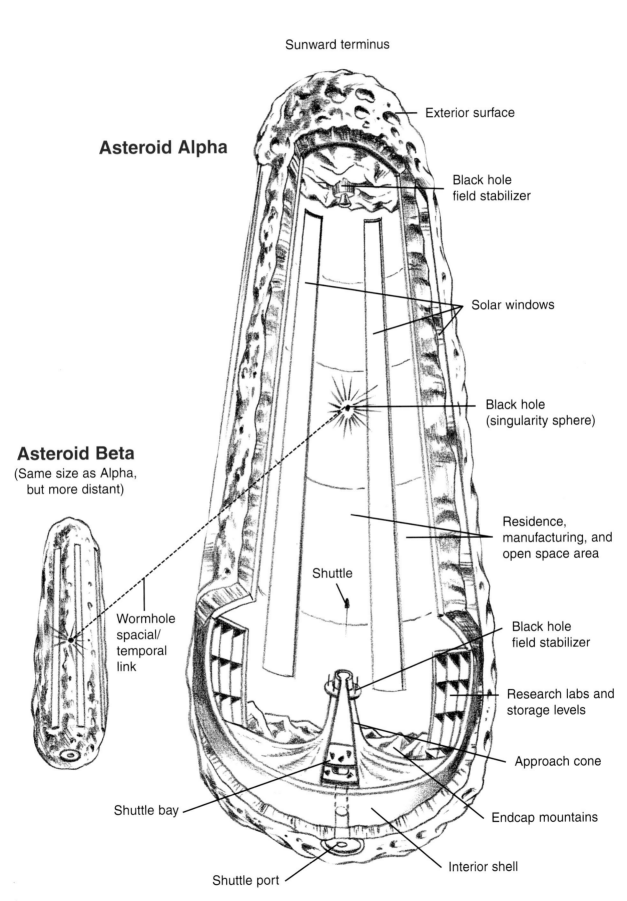

Sunward terminus

Exterior surface

Asteroid Alpha

Black hole field stabilizer

Solar windows

Black hole (singularity sphere)

Asteroid Beta
(Same size as Alpha, but more distant)

Residence, manufacturing, and open space area

Shuttle

Wormhole spacial/ temporal link

Black hole field stabilizer

Research labs and storage levels

Approach cone

Shuttle bay

Endcap mountains

Shuttle port

Interior shell

TRANSCRIBER'S OBSERVATIONS ON EXPLORING DEEP TIME

What Is Deep Time?

"Jon is always explaining how old things are," Neesha once wrote in the Diaries, "but all those zeros just make my brain numb." That makes for a pretty good definition of Deep Time—a point in time so long ago (or so far in the future) that just thinking about it paralyzes your mind. Still, like a voyager on the high seas, a time traveler must at least have a feeling for the size of the medium he or she is navigating to understand the history of Earth.

One million (1,000,000) is a large, awe-inspiring number. There are about half a million words in the English language. The city of Rome was founded about a million days ago. A million tons of raisins are produced annually, worldwide. Yet it takes a thousand million to make a billion.[2] Jon once said to Neesha: "Count to a billion, twerp, one second per number, and I'll come back for you in thirty-one years and six months."

Earth is 4.5 billion years old. It would take two lifetimes to count that high. Fortunately, the Olifees only traveled back 800 million years into Deep Time. You could count that high in just twenty-five years!

The work of two 19th-century geologists, James Hutton and Charles Lyell, helps us understand Deep Time. They recognized several important things:

1. The forces of erosion (mostly wind and water), which gradually tear down mountains and wash them into the sea, act at essentially the same rate now as they did in the past.

Sir Charles Lyell

2
Except in Great Britain and Germany, where a billion equals a million million.

The abyss from which the men of science should recoil is that of ignorance ...
—James Hutton

Dr. James Hutton

2. Rocks formed in the deep oceans remelt deep within the earth and eventually rise again as new mountains (in a process called uplift), which in turn are eroded and washed back into the sea.

3. You can see the boundaries between periods of uplift and erosion where streams have cut through rock to reveal layers of rocks tilted in different directions.

How Is Deep Time Measured?

Jon once told Neesha: "Deep Time is measured two ways: relative dating and absolute dating—and it's got nothing to do with boyfriends. Relative dating is when you know Rock A is older than Rock B because Rock A was found underneath Rock B. For a real-life example: If you never clean your room, the underwear at the bottom of your clothes pile is older than the underwear on top. Of course, if you go rooting around in the pile looking for a Hershey bar, you may mix things up, and that happens in nature too. Rocks get folded and buckled, earthquakes cause rock layers to split and slide past one another, and molten rock, like a melted candy bar, may seep between layers.

"Now pretend you don't clean your room for years. Your old toys can help mark the layers of clothes and junk. Baby toys at the bottom, then dolls and play dishes, then Virtual Game chips near the top. Animal and plant fossils show the same thing in nature. Because animals and plants change over time, fossils of a certain species are only found in rocks of a certain age—give or take a few million years. Common fossils found only in certain rock layers are called index fossils.

"Absolute dating is like having a clock that measures the length of time it takes one element to turn into another. Pretend half your ice-cream sundae turns into spinach every hour. If I looked at your sundae and a quarter of it was spinach, I'd know you've been flapping your lips at Landra for half an hour. In nature, certain unstable elements decay into

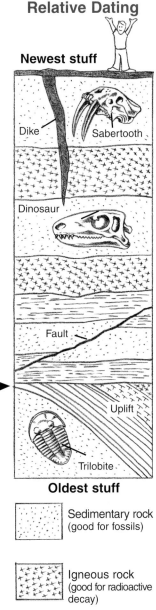

Relative Dating

Newest stuff

Dike · Sabertooth

Dinosaur

Fault

Erosion happened here

Uplift

Trilobite

Oldest stuff

Sedimentary rock (good for fossils)

Igneous rock (good for radioactive decay)

Absolute Dating

Potassium-40 (K^{40}) changes by radioactive decay into argon-40 (Ar^{40}). Half the potassium changes to argon in 1.3 billion years. Measuring the amount of argon in a sample allows scientists to calculate the age of the sample.

Absolute Dating

Time: 0 years

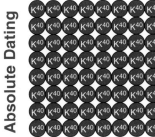

Time: 1.3 billion years

Time: 2.6 billion years

Time: 3.9 billion years

more stable ones very slowly by throwing off parts of their atoms. Talk to Landra for 1.3 billion years and half the potassium-40 created in volcanic rock will change into argon-40. Try it, little grub, I know you can do it!"

The time it takes half of a radioactive element to change into something else is its half-life. Because different elements have vastly different half-lives, some, like carbon-14, can be used to measure relatively short intervals (thousands or tens of thousands of years), and others, like potassium-40 and argon-40, can be used to measure the longest periods in Earth's history. The following chart summarizes some of the most useful "atomic clocks":

Unstable Element	Half-life (yrs.)	End Product	Used to Date
Uranium-238	4,500,000,000	Lead-206 & Helium-4	Coral, mollusks
Uranium-235	710,000,000	Lead-207 & Helium-4	Limestones
Thorium-232	15,000,000,000	Lead-208 & Helium-4	
Rubidium-87	50,000,000,000	Strontium-87	Igneous rocks
Potassium-40	1,300,000,000	Argon-40 & Calcium-40	or minerals
Carbon-14	5,730	Nitrogen-14	Wood, charcoal
			bone, carbonate

Other techniques for absolute dating include:

1. **Fission track dating:** High-energy decay products in uranium create microscopic tracks in a crystal lattice. To compute the age of a material, scientists compare the number of tracks present in a sample of that material to the number of tracks produced when uranium is decayed by a neutron field in the lab.
2. **Dendrochronology:** To compute the age of a site, scientists compare the number and size of tree rings in a wood sample associated with that site to ring samples from old living trees whose age is known. This only works for sites no more than a few thousand years old.
3. **Historical records:** Although recorded dates only go back a few thousand years, scientists can use them to help check the accuracy of carbon-14 and tree-ring dates.

Some complications with absolute dating:

1. With uranium decay, outside lead may contaminate the sample, making a site look older than it is.

2. In the potassium-argon method, argon, a gas, sometimes leaks out of the sample, making a site look younger than it is.

3. If rocks get remelted, atomic clocks get reset, so you have to find samples from geologically stable sites.

4. Because the quantity of decay products is often very small, measurements must be extremely accurate.

5. Decay products must not be reactive with other minerals and chemicals, or they won't be around for measuring millions of years later.

6. Because fossils are not often found in the igneous rocks used for absolute dating, their age must often be bracketed by dated igneous layers above and below them.

Help! Where's the math teacher?

Actual formula for calculating age:

$$t = 1/\lambda \ \ln(1 + D/p)$$

t = age of rock, λ = decay constant, ln = natural logarithm (log to base e)
D = number of atoms of decay product today
p = number of atoms of parent isotope today

A huge lion with fangs that would have
scared Dracula limped out from behind
a scrubby tree.

— Neesha

Teratorns and Tar Pits

Jump 1: Late Pleistocene, 20,000 years B.P.[1]

Day 1: Entry by Jon Olifee

When we accelerated through the wormhole I closed my eyes and waited to die. There was this adrenaline-maxed feeling I can't really describe, like I was being squashed and stretched at the same time. It didn't last long. We popped out of the wormhole, except it was the hole in Asteroid Beta! Alpha was in sight, but there were no military ships anywhere. Earth was nearby, hanging in space like a blue-white marble.

All of us huddled around the viewscreens as the shuttle put itself into a low orbit around Earth. When we crossed the terminator[2] we knew Earth wasn't the same. No city lights twinkled in the dark. The continents looked like mysterious blue-black blobs beneath the clouds, and the "North Pole" had gone crazy! Ice covered Canada and North America's Great Lakes. Dad said we must be seeing Earth during one of its ice ages.

When we got closer to the surface I could see that the shapes of the continents seemed odd. The North American continent extended farther into both the Atlantic Ocean and the Gulf of Mexico and the Florida penninsula looked more like a fat thumb than a finger. The California coastline looked about the same as I remembered, but as the shuttle skimmed over what should have been Los Angeles, I saw only what seemed to be an endless brown-and-green plain peppered with streams, clumps of trees, and scrubby bushes. We landed near a thicket of trees clustered around a small lake.

Our passenger bubble

---

[1] B.P. stands for "before present."

[2] The shadow line between day and night.

Day 2: Entry by Neesha Olifee

Mom's afraid to get too far away from the shuttle. Who knows when the "bug-bots" might launch it again?! Dad and Jon looked around a little this morning. They spooked some deer that were eating in the forest. Out on the plains near the lake they saw a huge herd of camels—real camels, humps and all! Dad said they were taller than he was. Dad and Jon also saw a pack of wolves, and Jon heard a lion roar—or so he says. That's when they came back to see if there were any weapons aboard the shuttle.

Guess what?! No weapons, but the bug-bots led us to a bonanza in one of the storage bays: a go-cart with six big wheels and a four-seat passenger bubble. Mom rigged up an alarm in case the shuttle engines start their warm-up sequence, so the four of us are going exploring tomorrow!

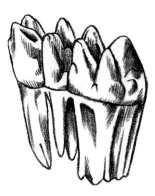

Mastodon molar tooth

Day 3: Letter from Neesha to her friend Landra

I'm still shaking, Landra. We just made it back in time! You may never see this letter, I know, but I have to talk to someone and I think about you all the time.

We were cruising in the bubblecart, see, looking at the camel and bison herds, when all of a sudden we were in this huge shadow. We looked up and this monster bird swooped over our heads. Mom's eyes bulged and she whispered, "That's a teratorn—they've been extinct for at least 10,000 years!" What's it eat? I wanted to ask when WHAM!—the bubblecart lurches to a stop and Dad says, "Uh oh."

He didn't see this tarry mess of stuff that was partly covered by dust. It really gooed up the front wheels. "Tar pits," Mom said. "We're stuck in tar pits—natural seeps of asphalt."

Mammoth tooth— one is a handful!

"Old Gimp"
He had a bad leg
(and a temper to match).

These camels always look like they're ready to spit on you!

The Teratorn perched close by in a gnarled old tree, and sat there looking at us like we had "Eat Me" written on our foreheads. Dad put the cart in full reverse and we started to back up a little. This tar stuff bubbled in spots and I saw all kinds of things that had gotten stuck: small birds, a lizard, and a bone that had belonged to something pretty big. I don't know how we got out of that junk, but we did.

We went up a hill to get around the tar and started down a different valley. But we came to another pit, this one with a house-sized cage of rib bones and a pair of curvy tusks rising up out of it. Bloody hunks of meat were still attached to the bones and a cloud of flies buzzed up as we got nearer, then settled down again on the meat. "Columbian mammoth," Mom whispered.

Then we heard this roar that made my scalp crawl. A huge lion with fangs that would have scared Dracula limped out from behind a scrubby tree. He looked scruffy and his front paws dripped tar, but he was nearly as big as our bubblecart and the muscles on his legs bulged when he walked. Later we joked and called him Old Gimp, but he nearly scared the goosebumps off my arm.

He didn't know what to make of us, but he snarled and limped a little closer. Dad revved the engine, and Old Gimp paused. But then five more lions slunk out of the bushes to see what was up.

"Ah, Greg …," Mom said, and then there was this incredible wailing sound that stopped the lions cold.

It was our alarm! The shuttle was warming up!

More later. Miss ya'.

—Love, Neesha

P.S. After the alarm, the lions loped off, like they had planned to leave anyway.

A teratorn gourmet

FOR 21ST-CENTURY EXPLORERS ...

The Olifees met a pride of *Smilodon*. Many of these cats were trapped in the La Brea tar pits. Saber-toothed predators arose several different times during the Cenozoic era among different groups of meat-eating animals. *Machairodus* evolved 50 million years earlier than *Smilodon*, during the Eocene epoch. At the same time, in South America a leopard-sized marsupial sabertooth known as *Thylacosmilus* prowled the forests. And 34 to 23 million years ago a predator called *Nimravus,* with slim, bladelike canine teeth, hunted in North America. Find pictures of as many saber-toothed cats as you can and plot when they lived on a timeline of the last 65 million years.

Technically, the 21st century is still part of an ice age, although we are currently experiencing a warm "intermission" period between southerly advances of large ice sheets. What do scientists believe causes ice ages? How might global warming from human activities affect the cycle of ice ages? Research these questions and write a report about what you learn.

Nine thousand years ago an eighteen-year-old woman was deliberately and carefully buried in the La Brea tar pits with some of the tools she used in life: a grinding stone, food-gathering tools, a ceremonial stone, shells, a hairpin carved from deer bone, and several atlatls (devices for throwing spears). A dog was also buried with her. Write a fictional story about the life of the "La Brea Woman."

REFERENCES

Agenbroad, Larry D. "Mammoth Site." *Natural History* 106, no. 9 (October 1997): 77–79.

Fenton, Carroll Lane, and Mildred Adams Fenton. *The Fossil Book*. New York: Doubleday, 1989. See especially pp. 619–625.

Janis, Christine. "The Sabertooth's Repeat Performances." *Natural History* 103, no. 4 (April 1994): 78–83. Contains information about many saber-toothed species.

Savage, R.J.G., and M. R. Long. *Mammal Evolution: An Illustrated Guide*. New York: Facts on File Publications, 1986.

Terra (Magazine of the Natural History Museum of Los Angeles County) 31, no. 1 (Fall 1992). Issue is devoted completely to the La Brea tar pits and contains more information about the "La Brea Woman."

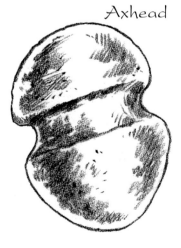

Axhead

We didn't see any people, but we found some of their stuff!

Hairpin

THE WORLD OF THE PRESENT AND JUMP 1

RESOURCES AND MAPS

The La Brea tar pits of Los Angeles contain perhaps the best selection of Ice Age creatures found anywhere. Fifty-six species of large mammals once lived there (compared to eleven today), along with Teratorns, a host of raptors (birds of prey), and a human population who mined the natural asphalt and used it to waterproof the roofs of their dwellings. Thanks to the efforts of George C. Page and others, you can see many of the discoveries from the tar pits at the George C. Page Museum of La Brea Discoveries, 5801 Wilshire Boulevard, Los Angeles, CA 90036. Phone: (323) 936-2230. Website: www.tarpits.org. Also visit the Natural History Museum of Los Angeles County, at 900 Exposition Blvd., Los Angeles, CA 90007. Phone: (323) 934-7243.

If you live close to South Dakota, visit the Mammoth Site in Hot Springs. Twenty-six thousand years ago Columbian and woolly mammoths fell into a natural, spring-fed sinkhole. In 1974 earth-moving equipment uncovered the first bones. Many bones were left in place, partially excavated, and a working museum was built around the site. Walkways allow visitors to see the fossils close up. National Geographic's *World* sponsors youth ages ten to sixteen in learning paleontological techniques, including excavation, mapping, and taking field notes. For more details contact the Mammoth Site, P.O. Box 606, Hot Springs, SD 57747-0606. Phone: (605) 745-6017. Website: www.mammothsite.com.

Cybister

Neat diving beetles!
They get stuck in the tar too.

La Brea Tar Pits
Downtown Los Angeles, California

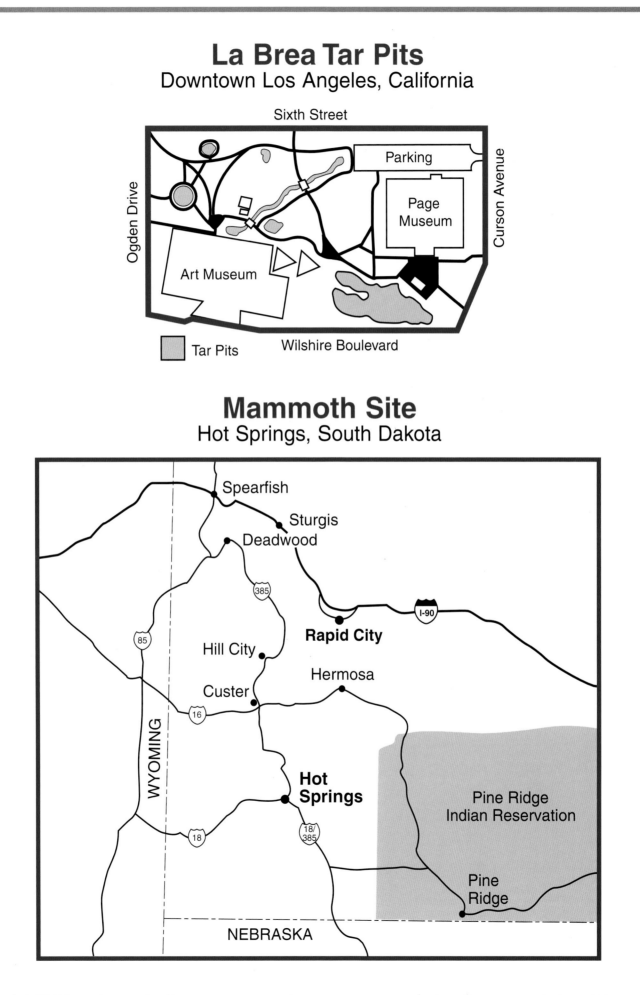

Mammoth Site
Hot Springs, South Dakota

Day 4: Letter from Neesha to Landra

Jon worries me sometimes. Lately he seems to think the only way we'll get back home is as fossils. It would be "kinda zifty," he says! I've got plans for my future, thank you very much. You and I are still going to be scientists on Callisto[3] someday and get some new alien "bugs" named after us. But anyway, just for laughs, here's Jon's "Five Ways to Fossilhood" plan (I figure Jon could meet the three requirements without hardly trying):

1. You usually have to have hard parts like bone or shell. (Jon's head, pound for pound, is harder than anything I know.)

2. It helps to get buried really fast to avoid decay. (I'm sure Jon could plan some way to stand under a falling mountain or something, especially if he knew it would keep maggots from munching on him. He hates bugs.)

3. You have to get lucky and die somewhere that's not going to change much in thousands or even millions of years. (Personally, Landra, I never use "die" and "lucky" in the same sentence.)

Once you meet these requirements, there are five ways to fossilhood:

1. **Freeze-dry/tar-baby/sap-sicle technique:** You can fall dead in a blizzard and let a glacier make a freezer-pop out of you, like some of those 10,000-year-old mammoths you hear about. Or, you can sit in a desert cave and dry up like one of those monster mummies. Or, you can step into a tar pit in the middle of July when it's nice and sticky. (Boy, Landra, do I know about that one!) Or, if you were as small as an insect, you could climb a pine tree and get globbed by a drop of sap, which, with time and pressure, would eventually harden into amber. Of

[3] A moon of Jupiter believed to have subsurface water.

Turtle shell

Hard stuff good for making fossils: Jon's head

course, except for the amber method, all these techniques are only good for a few tens of thousands of years. (The amber method wouldn't work for Jon anyway, so what's the use?)

2. Get petrified: This means get turned to stone. (Sounds perfect for Jon. I think he's always hoped someone would make a statue of him someday.) To do this, tie yourself to a concrete surfboard and jump into a lake. With all that weight, you'll get buried fast in the muck at the bottom of the lake. After your body rots, water will seep through the layers of muck, which later will turn hard as more muck piles on top. The water carries minerals that clog up the small canals in your bones, like sugar water evaporating in a soda straw. Sometimes the bone itself gets replaced by other minerals, sometimes not. Wood can get petrified this way. Dinosaurs too.

1.

Another technique is to get buried in hot lava from a volcano. This happens to trees a lot. The trees eventually rot away after the lava cools, and the cavities get filled by minerals. When the lava gets worn away, what's left looks like tree bark on the outside, but is just pretty rock on the inside.

3. Get carbonized: (I don't think Jon might would like this one, but it's a good way to get preserved if you don't mind looking like black road-kill.) Like getting petrified, you usually have to fall into a lake or swamp, but this time bacteria work on you as you get steeped with mineralized water. You also get slow-cooked and squashed as sediments pile up on top of you. (I think Jon used to

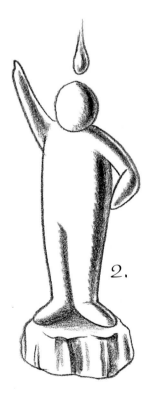

2.

3.

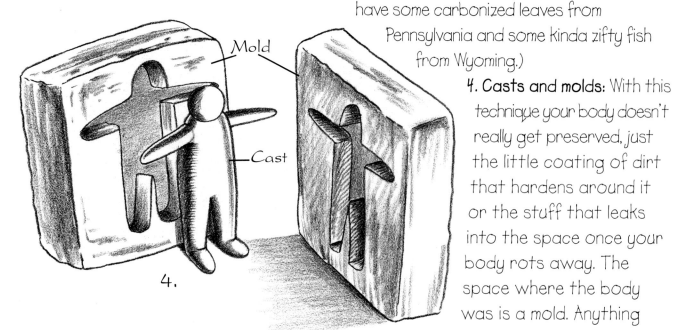

Mold

Cast

4.

have some carbonized leaves from Pennsylvania and some kinda zifty fish from Wyoming.)

4. **Casts and molds:** With this technique your body doesn't really get preserved, just the little coating of dirt that hardens around it or the stuff that leaks into the space once your body rots away. The space where the body was is a mold. Anything that seeps inside and hardens is a cast. Welcome to nature's pottery class!

5. **Trace fossils:** Trace fossils are just things and marks that living things leave behind: tracks, tunnels, and poop are good examples. If you want to sound smart, talk about coprolites—that's fossil poop. Ancient algae that grew in the oceans before there were animals around to eat them created big mounds of limestone called stromatolites. That's another good word. (You know, Landra, I wonder how many pop cans and old sneakers will become trace fossils?)

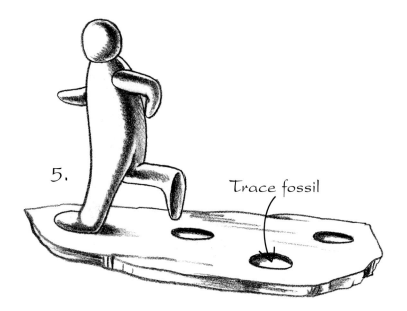

5.

Trace fossil

This morning I saw eyes in the forest.
—Neesha

Jungle Disaster

Jump 2: Early Eocene, 51 million years B.P.

Day 1: Entry by Jon Olifee

Cedrelospermum

Hackberry

The shuttle hustled us away from Ice Age California and back into space. Asteroids Alpha and Beta quickly grew from two bright specks on the viewscreens into the huge crater-pocked "moons" we knew them as. I would have sold my meteor collection to see Colonel Fasee's ships, but no such luck. The shuttle arced toward Asteroid Alpha and sped through the access port that led to the wormhole. We all held hands. Dad said something stupid like "Hang on."

We felt that whole squashed-stretched thing again, popped out of Asteroid Beta, and zoomed back to Earth. I hardly recognized it. The continents were bunched up toward the North Pole, a land bridge hooked North America to Europe and Australia to Antarctica, and there wasn't a sign of ice anywhere! In fact, green seemed to stretch from sea to sea.

The shuttle dropped quickly. We seemed to be headed toward three large lakes. "My paleo chip[1] recognizes this," Mom said. "Three huge lakes existed near the Colorado, Wyoming, and Utah borders about 50 million years ago."

Balloon vines

"Look at those unbroken miles of jungle," Dad said.

Neesha whined about feeling sick.

The shuttle shook until our teeth rattled as we sliced through dark storm clouds. We couldn't see the ground anymore. The cabin lights strobed a couple of times. If we hadn't been strapped in good, we might not have survived the crash.

[1] Some sort of databank implanted in Miriam's brain, probably a common occupational accessory in the 22nd century.

Macginitiea (sycamore relative)

Day 2: Letter from Neesha to Landra

Forget yesterday. Everybody thought we were going to be here for good and nobody won the smiley-face award—least of all Jon. Besides, I couldn't help where I threw up.

This morning I saw eyes in the forest. Big, round, yellow ones that peeked around the trunk of a tree. But I blinked, and the eyes were gone. All I could see through the mist were big palm fronds that looked kind of like sad, drooping hands.

Then I forgot about that because the bug-bots poured out from everywhere and started to form into what we called fix-bots. The fix-bots zoomed out of the shuttle, and so did we. While we huddled by a tree, the fix-bots bunched around the shuttle's buckled nose and landing gear. Some 'bots scooped rocks, dirt, and other stuff into cavities inside other 'bots. Somehow these receiver 'bots processed the stuff into new shuttle parts. Dad thinks they must run on super-efficient solar cells of some kind.

Once we realized the fix-bots would take a while to finish, we decided to explore. Mom rigged up her alarm again and Dad found some sonic guns that he thinks will scare any dangerous animals. I hope so. We plan to follow a game trail to Fossil Lake—at least that's what Mom's paleo chip calls it.

Wish you could come!

—Neesha

This feather factory was seven feet tall and had a head as big as a horse and the attitude of an eagle. We kept out of this birdie's way!

—Neesha

Diatryma

Tons of these on the lake. This one liked our "trough lunch" so much we named her "Greasy."

Presbyornis

Day 2, about 1200 hours: Entry by Neesha Olifee

The lake is great, even if it was *muggy* and *buggy* getting here. Strange ducks are feeding near the reeds, keeping one eye out for the crocodiles. Me too. We scared some long-legged shorebirds when we first entered the clearing near the shore, but they came back and are spearing fish with their beaks.

We had a scare on the way. Four hyena-like things were munching on something, and they weren't about to move. They scattered when Dad popped off the sonic gun, but we could hear them now and then close by. Then we heard some loud snorts and lots of snapping branches and rustling leaves. This huge head—as long as I am tall—poked out of the bushes. It squinted at us with tiny eyes. It had six head horns, a rhino's body, and a pair of tusks that looked like saber teeth! Good thing it turned out to be a veggie-beast and decided we weren't lunch. We let him have the trail to himself.

Day 4: Entry by Neesha Olifee

Early this morning, before the others were up, I was outside the *Chronos* (that's what we christened the shuttle after the fix-bots were done with repairs). I figured we'd leave soon, and I was still curious about those eyes I had seen. I sat real still and quiet. And you know what? Those eyes belonged to an odd little monkey. It looked at me through the branches of a huge willow tree. Neither of us made a sound.

We had a stare-down for at least a couple of minutes. For a while it seemed like I could almost fall into those big, yellow eyes. Then the monkey scratched its head just like Jon does, and I laughed. The monkey ran away before I could say goodbye.

Fix-bot

Part processor bot

FOR 21ST-CENTURY EXPLORERS ...

Neesha's "monkey" may have been *Notharctus* or *Smilodectes,* one of a dozen or so common early primates that developed in what is now North America, Europe, and Asia. Find out why they disappeared in North America 35 million years ago and write a report about what you learn.

Find out the scientific name and the size of the saber-toothed "veggie-beast" described by Neesha. Hint: It's a kind of uintathere.

Some bird species that appeared during the early Eocene epoch would look familiar today. You might mistake some of them for modern-day shorebirds and ducks. One, however, was a fierce, six-foot-tall predator called *Diatryma,* which probably terrorized many early mammals. Write a short report about this fearsome, flightless bird.

Check out Fossil Butte National Monument. The monument is located near Kemmerer, Wyoming, and the fossil fish and other creatures found there once lived in and near Wyoming's Fossil Lake. Contact the monument at:

Fossil Butte National Monument
P.O. Box 527 • Kemmerer, WY 83101
Phone: (307) 877-4455 • Website: www.nps.gov/fobu/

REFERENCES

Feduccia, Alan. *The Origin and Evolution of Birds.* New Haven, CT, and London: Yale University Press, 1996. Chapter 6 deals with *Diatryma* and other flightless birds of the Eocene epoch.

Grande, Lance. "Paleontology of the Green River Formation, with a Review of the Fish Fauna." Bulletin no. 63. Cheyenne, WY: Pioneer Printing, 1980. Technical, but the most complete reference to Green River Formation fossils—those fossils preserved in lake sediments from 40–50 million years ago in portions of Colorado, Wyoming, and Utah.

Lageson, David, and Darwin Spearing. *Roadside Geology of Wyoming.* Missoula, MT: Mountain Press Publishing, 1988.

McPhee, John. *Basin and Range.* New York: Noonday Press, Farrar, Straus & Giroux, 1981. Classic general reference to basin and range geology; very well written.

Ostrom, John, et al. *The Age of Mammals.* New Haven, CT: Yale University Printing Service, 1993. Check the USGS website for this booklet and other publications at www.usgs.gov/educatoin/edulist.html.

Zimmer, Carl. "Terror Take Two." *Discover* 18, no. 6 (June 1997): 68–74. The latest thoughts on the "terror bird"—*Diatryma.*

This guy was cute in an ugly sort of way. You can tell by his mouth he was a surface feeder.

Diplomystus

Several booklets and other publications about the Fossil Lake area are available through:

Dinosaur Nature Association
1291 E. Highway 40
Vernal, UT 84078
Phone: (800) 845-3466
Website: www.dinosaurnature.com

RESOURCES AND MAPS

As the Rocky Mountains began to rise 70 million years ago, just after the mega-extinction that destroyed the dinosaurs, deep sedimentary basins that helped preserve a detailed record of life in the Cenozoic era developed in northern Wyoming and elsewhere. Large lakes existed for more than 17 million years where the modern-day states of Utah, Colorado, and Wyoming meet. Large fish kills sometimes occurred in Fossil Lake when oxygen-poor bottom water with excesses of hydrogen sulfide from decomposing animals periodically "turned over," destroying many fish in the upper layer of the lake. And nearby volcanoes caused ashfall kills from time to time. Many kinds of animals and plants were preserved, including reptiles, amphibians, bats, birds, insects, crustaceans, palm fronds, leaves, tree wood, and balloon vines.

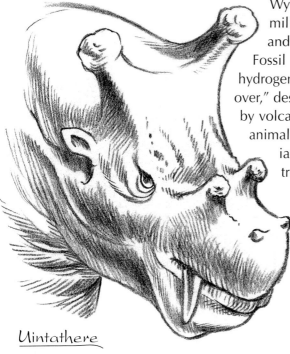

Uintathere

You can dig your own fossils (for an hourly fee) at Ulrich Fossil Gallery in Kemmerer, Wyoming. Owners Karl and Shirley Ulrich are very accommodating and offer discounts for school groups. Visit them at:

Ulrich Fossil Gallery
Fossil Station #308
Kemmerer, WY 83101
Phone: (307) 877-6466

Also try:
Tynskey's Fossil Fish
201 Beryl St.
Kemmerer, WY 83101
Phone: (307) 877-6885 (ask for Jim or Karen Tynskey)

THE EOCENE WORLD

Fossil Butte National Monument and Kemmerer Area

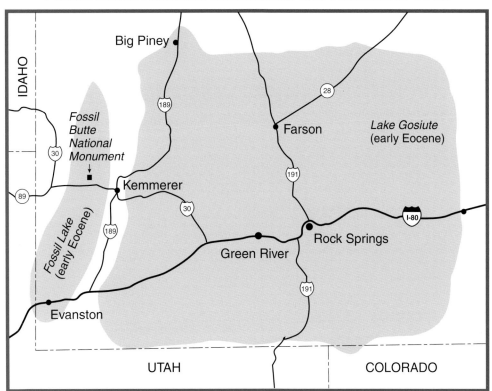

You can dig fossil insects and plants (for an hourly fee) at:

> Florissant Fossil Quarry
> P.O. Box 126
> Florissant, CO 80816
> Phone: (719) 748-1002 (ask for Nancy
>   Anderson) or (719) 748-3275 (ask for
>   Toni Clare)

Other Cenozoic-era fossil sites in the United States include:

> Agate Fossil Beds National Monument
> P.O. Box 27
> Gering, NE 69341

> Badlands National Park
> P.O. Box 6
> Interior, SD 57750

> Florissant Fossil Beds National Monument
> P.O. Box 185
> Florissant, CO 80816

> Hagerman Fossil Beds National Monument
> 963 Blue Lakes Blvd., Suite 1
> Twin Falls, ID 82551

The Ashfall Fossil Beds in Antelope County, Nebraska, preserve fossil rhinos, horses, camels, and birds that died 10 million years ago after a volcanic eruption. The following University of Nebraska State Museum website has more information: www.museum.unl.edu/research/vertpaleo/ashfall.html.

Soon-to-be-scrambled eggs.
—Neesha

Mother Trouble

Jump 3: Late Cretaceous, 68 million years B.P.

Day 1: Entry by Jon Olifee

Be it here recorded: Today I became the first person ever to touch a living <u>Triceratops</u>! Smelled 'em, too. They clear their bowels real fast when they're scared.

We saw thousands of them from the air as the shuttle cruised over rolling, tree-speckled plains. The herds raised clouds of dust when they ran away from our passing shadow. We saw armored, knob-tailed ankylosaurs and speedy ostrich dinos[1] too. The shuttle landed on high ground not far from a pair of sixty-foot-tall hadrosaurs munching pine boughs at the edge of a small forest.

By the time we got outside, the hadros had disappeared into the woods, but a hundred yards away in a little gully Dad and I found a <u>Triceratops</u> cow with two calves. Actually, I kind of stumbled into one of the calves, which were sleeping. The calf was as big as a large boulder, but it felt warm and had big, bumpy warts on its hide. The calf bleated, jumped up, and—when it saw us—dropped a load. By then mamma <u>Triceratops</u> had caught our scent. She swung her frilled head from side to side and snorted. We retreated and trotted back to the shuttle.

Day 1: Letter from Neesha to Landra

The bug-bots assemble into what Dad calls the "grease trough" to feed us. Yummy-sounding, isn't it, Landra? Not only is the food weird, the trough machine makes you talk or solve little puzzles—like matching shapes and symbols and stuff—before it chucks out the people-chow. Makes you feel like a lab rat. Sometimes I talk to it in Pig Latin. I hope it blows a circuit.

I've also got a great idea for breakfast.

—Neesha

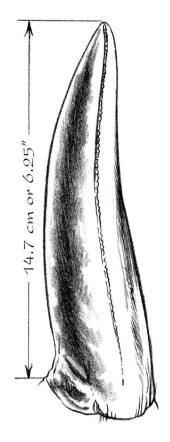

14.7 cm or 6.25"

<u>T. rex</u> tooth! Just like a steak knife!

Front
Back

<u>Triceratops</u> tooth. Neesha found a bunch of these.

Cute triceros, huh!

---
[1] Ornithomimosaurs of some kind.

Day 2: Entry by Jon Olifee

Neesha dragged me outside early this morning. Said she was tired of eating "McAlien Surprise" meals. We followed a game trail into the woods, but I didn't like the size of some of the tracks I saw. Just before I was about to drag her back by the hair, she pointed to a spot near a clump of ferns. "Soon-to-be-scrambled eggs," she said.

Before I could even tell her it was a bad idea, we heard a noise to our left, and this long-legged, long-necked ostrich dino trotted out of the bushes. She had dark, iridescent feathers on her neck and body and long arms that ended in three-fingered claws. She cocked her head just like a bird and gave us a cold stare. I gave Neesha a shove back along the trail away from the nest. Mammasaur shrieked and trotted our way, but fortunately stopped when she got to her nest.

When we got back to the Chronos, Mamma Olifee wasn't so happy either. There must be some sort of "Mom Schools," where all moms learn how to shake their heads, snort, and shriek.

Parasaurolophus:
The males sound like lovesick moose near their breeding grounds.

Day 3: Entry by Neesha Olifee

We had a campfire last night, just like when I was a kid. Mom made a fire near a big rock close to the shuttle, using some dry wood collected from what Dad calls the Monkey Puzzle Tree Forest.[2] At dusk, big male hadrosaurs with long, curved horns on their heads bugled close by. It seemed like I could almost feel the sound in my toes. Mom said that the hadros were *Parasaurolophus*

This ankylosaur had a personality as prickly as its hide.

[2] Monkey puzzle trees are ancient conifers that survived into the 21st century in South America and Australia.

and that the head horns were hollow and helped to make the bugling sound.

The stars looked close enough to touch. We saw a bunch of meteors flame out across the sky. As you can imagine, Jon was gaga about that. Mom said that sometime soon an asteroid six miles long would strike Earth, leading to the end of the dinosaurs' reign. I got a little nervous until I found out that "sometime soon" for Mom was a few million years.

Day 4: Entry by Jon Olifee

Dad and I were outside this morning cleaning up the campfire area when the ground shook. Whatever it was even made ripples in a couple of puddles nearby. Dad looked kinda pale. He said this reminded him of an old 2-D movie he had seen once. He herded me into the shuttle with everyone else.

The shaking got worse. Pretty soon the shuttle engines started up and we lifted off. Then we saw it: a real live T. rex—two stories tall with six-inch daggers for teeth. The shuttle circled him once before leaving, and he gave a roar that made the hairs at the back of my neck stand up.

For the next few sleep cycles Neesha jumped a foot out of her bed whenever I growled in her ear.

Monkey puzzle tree: too prickly to be a good "climber"!

Dinner is served!
yuk

FOR 21ST-CENTURY EXPLORERS ...

Triceratops is perhaps the most well known of a group of rhino-like dinosaurs called ceratopsians, which had horns and head frills. Perhaps the strangest was *Styracosaurus*, with its six head spikes and a huge nose horn more than twenty inches long. Look up and draw as many of the following species as you can find: *Centrosaurus, Monoclonius, Avaceratops, Brachyceratops, Pachyrhinosaurus, Einiosaurus,* and *Achelosaurus*. Besides defense, what other function might elaborate horns and frills have had for ceratopsians?

The fictional character Indiana Jones may have been based on the real-life paleontologist Roy Chapman Andrews, who discovered important late Cretaceous–age dinosaurs in the Gobi Desert of Mongolia in the 1920s and 30s. Write a short biography on Mr. Andrews.

Many scientists now believe that a large asteroid collided with Earth 65 million years ago in what is now the Yucatan, a peninsula of southeastern Mexico. What is the name of the crater that the asteroid created? How was it discovered? Why did scientists start looking for it? Aside from the asteroid, what other factors may have led to the ensuing mega-extinction? Research these questions and write a report about what you learn.

REFERENCES

Dinosaurs in General

Gore, Rick. "Dinosaurs." *National Geographic* 183, no. 1 (January 1993): 2–53.

Jenkins, John T., and Jannice L. Jenkins. *Colorado's Dinosaurs*. Denver, CO: Colorado Geological Survey, 1993.

Novacek, Michael. *Dinosaurs of the Flaming Cliffs*. New York: Alfred A. Knopf, 1996. Modern-day excavations in the Gobi Desert.

Sereno, Paul C. "Africa's Dinosaur Castaways." *National Geographic* 190, no. 6 (June 1996): 106–119.

Webster, Donovan. "Dinosaurs of the Gobi." *National Geographic* 190, no. 1 (July 1996): 70–89.

Horned Dinosaurs

Dodson, Peter. *The Horned Dinosaurs*. Princeton, NJ: Princeton University Press, 1996.

Kirkland, James. "Horns of Plenty." *Earth* 6, no. 6 (December 1997): 26–31.

"Prehistoric Sounds." *Earth* 7, no. 2 (April 1998): 14. Information about *Parasaurolophus's* head crest. (Reported by Gretel Schueller in "Earth News")

Roy Chapman Andrews and Other Dino Hunters

Lanham, Url. *The Bone Hunters.* New York: Dover Publications, 1973.

Rogers, Katherine. *The Sternberg Fossil Hunters—A Dinosaur Dynasty.* Missoula, MT: Mountain Press Publishing, 1991.

Wallace, Joseph. *The American Museum of Natural History's Book of Dinosaurs and Other Ancient Creatures.* New York: Simon and Schuster, 1994.

Wilford, John Noble. The Riddle of the Dinosaurs. New York: Alfred A. Knopf, 1985.

Dinosaur Extinction

Alvarez, Walter. *T. rex and the Crater of Doom.* Princeton, NJ: Princeton University Press, 1997.

Archibald, David J. *Dinosaur Extinction and the End of an Era.* New York: Columbia University Press, 1996.

THE CRETACEOUS WORLD

RESOURCES AND MAPS

If any single dinosaur fossil could bring to life the essence of the creature from which it was formed, it might be the "dinosaur mummy" found by Charles Sternberg and his sons in 1908. A fossilized hadrosaur, *Edmontosaurus,* was found sixty-five miles from Lusk, Wyoming, at the end of a long season of field work. After the dinosaur died, its body somehow dried out quickly, without being torn apart by scavengers, and became covered with sand.

Bumps, or tubercles, of various sizes and patterns covered the dinosaur's hide, showing that dinosaur skin was not scaly. The hadrosaur's soft tissue, including the stomach and its contents, had been preserved. It was determined that the dinosaur ate pine needles, bark, cones, and other dry-land vegetation. Douglas Preston wrote: "Lying on its back, with gaping rib cage and grinning skull … the specimen looks like a partially decomposed carcass—one can almost smell it."[3] You can still see the Sternbergs' find at the American Museum of Natural History, Central Park West at 79th St., New York, NY 10024. Phone: (212) 769-5100. Website: www.amnh.org. Also read "The Dinosaur Mummy" by Gary Raham in *Highlights for Children,* February 2000.

---

[3] Rogers, Katherine. *The Sternberg Fossil Hunters: A Dinosaur Dynasty.* Missoula, MT.: Mountain Press, 1991: 116. (They quoted *Natural History,* January 1982.)

Dinosaur Sites in Four Western States

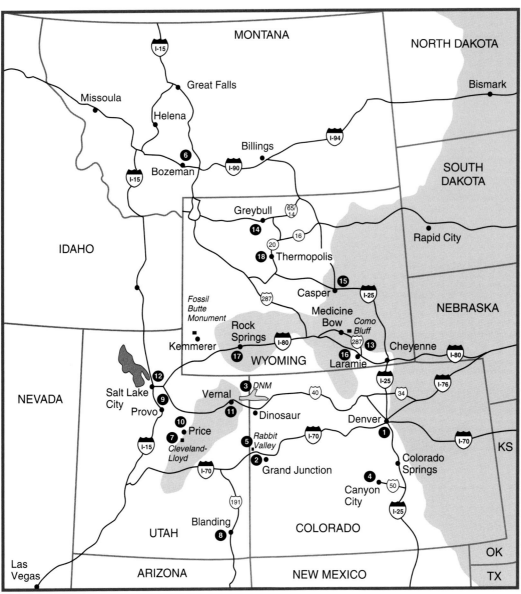

COLORADO
1. Denver Museum of Nature & Science
   Dinosaur Ridge (in Morrison)
2. Devils Canyon Science & Learning Center
   Museum of Western Colorado
   Riggs Hill Trail
3. Dinosaur National Monument
4. Garden Park Paleontological Society
5. Rabbit Valley Quarry and Trail

MONTANA
6. Museum of the Rockies

UTAH
7. Cleveland-Lloyd Quarry
8. Dinosaur Museum
9. Earth Science Museum
10. CEU Prehistoric Museum
11. Utah Field House of
    Natural History
12. Utah Museum of Natural History

WYOMING
13. Como Bluff
14. Greybull Museum
15. Tate Mineralogical Museum
16. University of Wyoming
    Geology Museum
17. Western Wyoming
    Community College Museum
18. Wyoming Dinosaur Center

Approximate location of Western Interior Seaway
74 million years ago.

In Colorado, Wyoming, and Montana you can find many fascinating Cretaceous-age creatures in the following places:

Denver Museum of Nature and Science
2001 Colorado Blvd.
Denver, CO 80205
Phone: (303) 370-6357
Website: www.dmns.org

Devil's Canyon Science and Learning Center
550 Crossroads Ct.
Fruita, CO 81521
Phone: (970) 858-7282

Garden Park Paleontological Society Dig Site
    and Display (Dinosaur Depot)
P.O. Box 313
Canon City, CO 81215-0313
Phone: (719) 269-7150
Website: www.dinosaurdepot.com

Museum of Western Colorado/Dinosaur Valley
P.O. Box 20000-5020
Grand Junction, CO 81502-5020
Phone: (970) 242-0971
Website: www.wcmuseum.org or
    www.dinodigs.org

Greybull Museum
325 Greybull St.
Greybull, WY 82462
Phone: (307) 765-2444

Como Bluff Site
c/o Medicine Bow Museum
P.O. Box 187
Medicine Bow, WY 83239
Phone: (307) 379-2383

University of Wyoming Geology Museum
P.O. Box 3006
Laramie, WY 82071-3006
Phone: (307) 766-4218

Wyoming Dinosaur Center
P.O. Box 868
Thermopolis, WY 80443
Phone: (307) 864-5522
Website: www.wyodino.org

Museum of the Rockies
Montana State University
600 W. Kagy Blvd.
Bozeman, MT 59717-0272
Phone: (406) 994-2251
Website: www.montana.edu/wwwmor/

A great organization for budding paleontologists is the Western Interior Paleontological Society (WIPS). They have an information-packed newsletter called *Trilobite Tales,* monthly meetings at the Denver Museum of Nature and Science, paleontology certification classes, volunteer opportunities, and great, inexpensive summer field trips. Contact WIPS at:
    Western Interior Paleontological Society
    P.O. Box 200011
    Denver, CO 80220-0011
    Website: www.wipsppc.com

Then, just about dawn, everyone woke
to growls and thrashings close by.
—Jon

The Monsters of Blue Lagoon

Jump 4: Middle Cretaceous, 110 million years B.P.

Day 1: Entry by Jon Olifee

As the shuttle got closer to Earth, the continents looked totally strange. Everyone wondered how far we'd jumped this time. Twenty thousand years the first trip, more than 50 million years on the second, then 68 million on the third. Mom wondered if this jump would show a pattern. The big question is, can we ever go forward again, maybe by entering the other wormhole first?

We're dropping toward the seaward edge of a big continent. Offshore there's a huge string of what Dad calls barrier islands--like the Atlantic and Gulf Coast islands in our century. Mom spotted a few flowers in a zoom scan. She says this means we're no farther back than the middle Cretaceous period at most. More dinosaurs! I'm ready.

Day 1, near sunset: Entry addendum by Neesha Olifee

Yeah, Jon's ready all right. Ready to get stepped on.

The shuttle came down near this mega-cosmic lagoon: it looked like some clear, blue-green eye full of wispy clouds. Pretty, as long as you stay clear of the crocodiles and keep an eye on whatever wanders out of the forest of odd pine trees, ferns, and pineapple-shaped things with droopy leaves.[1] We saw a herd of long-necked dinos of some kind way down the beach. Some were wading in the lagoon. Flocks of what looked like white birds scattered when the big guys moved, then resettled on the dinos' backs. Dad looked through some binocular things he found and said

---

[1] Most likely cycads.

the "birds" were really white-furred pterosaurs, probably looking for juicy, hide-crawling insects. Yum!

So we're all looking down the beach, not far from the forest, when Jon says, "Quit pokin' me, grub." I told the micro-brain I wasn't anywhere near him. Jon turned around and let out a yelp. A baby long-neck was looking for something to eat in his back pocket.

Then things got crazy. The ground shook. Twigs snapped and bushes started moving. Something made a loud bellow behind us. One majorly big, long-necked, crinkly skinned 'saur with tree-trunk-sized legs came crashing through the under-brush onto the beach. We ran like our butts were on fire. But mamma dino just wanted her baby. She nudged the kid with her snout and pushed it toward the herd. By the time we got the sand and twigs out of our shoes, they were at the far end of a long line of foot-prints.

This is one of the world's first flowers— looks kinda like a magnolia.

Day 3: Entry by Jon Olifee

Everyone was too tired to make log entries yesterday. Lots of strange noises from the forest kept everybody tossing and turning all night. And the shuttle kind of hummed like a one-tune idiot in a hot shower. Dad thought it was in some sort of alert mode.

Then, just about dawn, everyone woke up to growls and thrashings close by. It sounded like one heck of a fight. When I stumbled into the control room, Neesha had her arms around Mom in a death grip and Dad was pointing at the aft viewscreen. A twelve-foot-tall thero-pod with tiger stripes and some kind of partly chewed-up crest on its head staggered toward us. It raised its head

This robber crab made his hideout in a fresh dino print.

and howled. Blood ran down one leg and turned the sand dark.

Then the shuttle actually talked to us. Sort of. It played back things we'd said to one another during jumps, and things we'd said to the grease troughs when we got our food rations. But the replayed messages came across in a way that was like a warning: "Hang on!" "No, you can't go outside now!" "Of course I mean it!" "Doors locked tight."

The beast outside didn't look too good. It glared at us for a minute, but then its eyes got glassy, its legs buckled, and it sort of rolled over on its side like our overweight house cat used to do. Mom said her paleo chip tentatively ID'd the creature: Acrocanthosaurus. We never did see what attacked him.

The acro was scary all right, but it was hard to watch him die. After he got too weak to growl and snap, a pack of Deinonychus moved in. They slit his belly real quick with their sickle-shaped toe claws. When they'd had their fill, smaller creatures stole bits of meat from the carcass and dragged them off to a safe distance. Mom's paleo chip couldn't recognize most of them. Dad finally blanked the aft viewscreen. I didn't mind. I concentrated on the view of the lagoon. Everything seemed so peaceful there. When I squinted my eyes, the wading long-necks almost looked like swans. I could still hear the pterosaurs' sad-seeming cries long after we'd left the lagoon and Cretaceous-age Earth behind.

Found this wierd pterosaur skull on the beach! Dad says the teeth show it was a fish-eater.
    —Jon

Stamens

"Fruit"

Acrocanthosaurus

FOR 21ST-CENTURY EXPLORERS ...

Near Glenrose, Texas, and the modern-day Paluxy River, dinosaurs left their tracks along an ancient lagoon. You can also find excellent trackways in New Mexico, Utah, and Colorado. Scientists can learn a great deal about dinosaur size, movement, and behavior from trackways. For example, by comparing footprint length to leg length for dinosaurs with complete skeletons, scientists know that the height of a dinosaur from foot to hip is four to five times the footprint length. Try some calculations on your own: If a dinosaur footprint is thirty centimeters long, what is the dinosaur's hip height? If that same dinosaur is two and a half times longer than its hip height, what is the minimum length of the dinosaur?

Casting Animal Tracks:

Find some animal tracks in the mud near a creek or lake. You can make copies of these prints, just as scientists make copies of dinosaur tracks.

You will need:

plaster of paris	plastic food container	thin cardboard
water	pocket knife	freezer tape
large spoon	scissors	thick shampoo

Directions:

1. Mix the plaster of paris in the food container according to package directions.
2. Spoon the plaster into one of the tracks, filling it to a depth of about an inch above the surrounding mud. Allow the plaster to harden for a couple of hours, then carefully lift the cake of plaster (called a cast) from the mud. Do not clean the cast at this point. Let it harden overnight, then clean off any excess mud the next day.
3. With the pocket knife (ask an adult for help), carefully trim the cast to a round shape.
4. Cut a four-inch-wide strip of cardboard long enough to encircle the cast. Wrap it around the cast and tape the edges together with freezer tape. You should have two or three inches of space above your track cast enclosed by the cardboard. Smear some thick shampoo on top of the cast.
5. Mix a new batch of plaster and fill the inside of the cardboard collar. Let the plaster harden overnight, then remove the cardboard and carefully separate the plaster cast from the plaster mold, which will now look like the original animal print.

Answer: Hip height (minimum) = 120 cm; maximum hip height = 150 cm. Minimum length is 2.5 x 120 cm = 300 cm.

REFERENCES

Czerkas, Sylvia J., and Stephen A. Czerkas. *Dinosaurs: A Global View.* New York: Mallard Press, 1991.

Encyclopedia of Dinosaurs. Lincolnwood, IL: Publications International, 1990.

Encyclopedia of Dinosaurs. New York: Academic Press, 1997.

Halls, Kelly Milner. *Dino-Trekking.* New York: John Wiley & Sons, 1996.

Lockley, Martin. *Tracking Dinosaurs.* New York: Cambridge University Press, 1991.

Russell, Dale A. *An Odyssey in Time: The Dinosaurs of North America.* Minocqua, WI: NorthWord Press, 1989.

Stein, Sara. *The Evolution Book.* New York: Workman Publishing, 1986.

Thomas, David A., and James O. Farlow. "Tracking a Dinosaur Attack." *Scientific American*, December 1997.

RESOURCES AND MAPS

Dinosaur tracks were first discovered near the Paluxy River by a young girl in 1909. They were confirmed to be dinosaur tracks by Roland Bird in 1938. You can see dinosaur tracks from the area near the Olifees' time jump at Dinosaur Valley State Park. For information contact:

Dinosaur Valley State Park
P.O. Box 396
Glenrose, TX 78043
Phone: (254) 897-4588
Website: www.cyberspacemuseum.com/n4_11.html

Dinosaur Ridge forms part of the hogbacks west of Denver near Morrison, Colorado. Dinosaur trackways there tilt up at a 45-degree angle and are easily accessed by road. In 1877, a school teacher named Arthur Lakes discovered huge dinosaur bones in this area. When he sent some of the fossils to two experts, Othniel Marsh and Edward Cope, he inadvertently started an intense, twenty-year competition between these two men to find the biggest and best dinosaur bones—a competition that became so bitter it was later referred to as the "Dinosaur Wars." For more information about dinosaur ridge, contact:

Dinosaur Ridge
P.O. Box 564
Morrison, CO 80465
Website: www.dinoridge.org

Original track

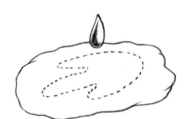

Pour on plaster

bottom of track

Remove cast and trim to shape

Replica of original print

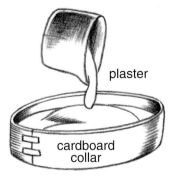

plaster

cardboard collar

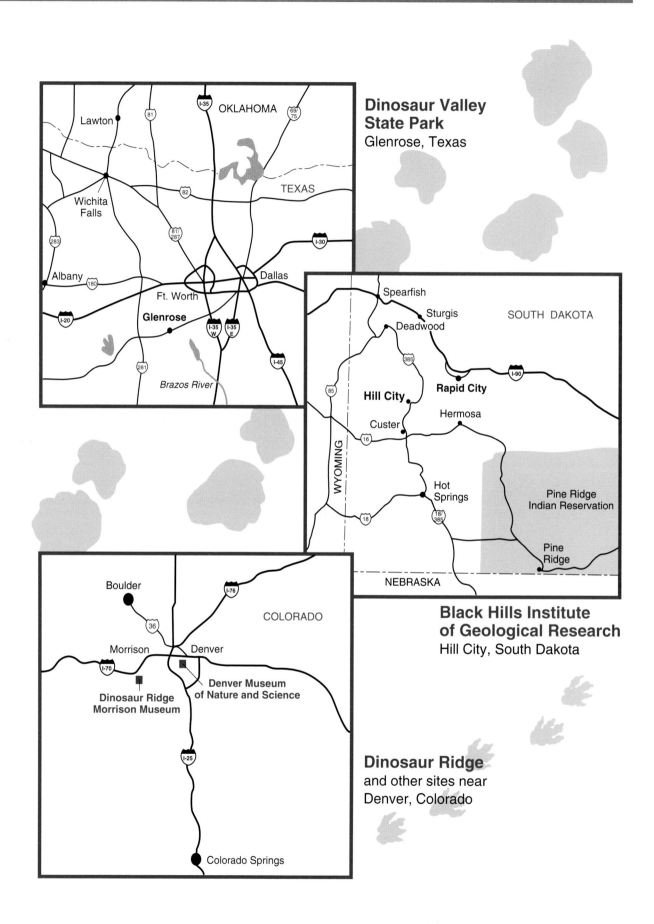

Dinosaur Valley State Park
Glenrose, Texas

Black Hills Institute of Geological Research
Hill City, South Dakota

Dinosaur Ridge
and other sites near Denver, Colorado

THE CRETACEOUS WORLD

Information on dinosaur trackways is also available at the following websites: www.emory.edu/Geoscience/html/dinotraces.htm and www.emory.edu/Geoscience/html/dinolinks.htm.

A hundred million years ago near what is now Ardmore, Oklahoma, an *Acrocanthosaurus* suffered severe injuries, presumably in a fight with a competitor. It sustained a punctured shoulder blade and several broken ribs, but survived to fight another day. Its fossil remains were eventually sold to the North Carolina State Museum of Natural Sciences in Raleigh. For more information check out: www.wmnh.com/wmgeoooo.htm.

The Black Hills Institute of Geological Research collects and reconstructs dinosaur fossils. See their exhibits at:

Black Hills Institute of Geological Research
217 Main St./P.O. Box 643
Hill City, SD 57745
Website: www.bhigr.com

The *T. rex,* Sue, originally discovered by The Black Hills Institute, was purchased at an auction in 1997 by Chicago's Field Museum and is now on display there. A complete exhibit hall built around this 90% complete fossil should be ready in 2003.

Field Museum of Natural History
Roosevelt Road at Lake Shore Drive
Chicago, IL 60605
Phone: (312) 922-9410

Also see the *National Geographic* article, "Debut Sue," Donovan Webster, *National Geographic,* vol. 197, No. 6, June 2000 p. 24–37.

It seemed like the end of the world—with no ark in
sight and the most bizarre parade of animals ever.
—Neesha

The Flood

Jump 5: Jurassic, 145 million years B.P.

Day 1: Entry by Neesha Olifee

Seemed like we hardly noticed the jump this time. Maybe we're getting used to this roller coaster. But Earth still looked so strange—most of the land was bunched up in one big continent. We could have been landing on Planet X for all I could tell.

The shuttle brought us down at night, which made everything look spooky. We followed a wide river that twisted like a silver snake in the moonlight. Eventually we landed on a big sandbar with its own miniforest of evergreens and tree ferns. Mom told us to rest for a couple of hours, so I better turn this flashlight off before Jon rats me out.

Day 1: Entry by Jon Olifee

A loud boom this morning got everybody's attention. Neesha got tangled in her bunk webbing[1] and I think Dad fell out of his--he was limping as we all piled into the control room and turned on the viewscreens. Before we could even ask what the blast of sound was, there was another. It sounded like a jet breaking the sound barrier right over our heads. When we could finally see outside, my jaw just about fell off.

A monster bull sauropod of some kind—at least as big as the shuttle—was giving us the evil eye and swaying his head back and forth on an unbelievably long neck. His forelegs were on the sandbar and his hindquarters were in the river—a long baseball throw away. Behind him a herd of his buddies were bellowing and making their way across the river. Then we saw the bull's

Diplodocus teeth look like pegs.

Brachiosaurus teeth look like spoons.

Lots of sauropod teeth on the beach!
　　　　　　—Jon

Brachiosaurus

---
[1] The shuttle beds were designed for zero-G conditions.

tail move. The end of it flicked in a blur and another crack of sound made us cover our ears. Dad said the tip of the tail was breaking the sound barrier.

The ship talked to us again. This time it made up its own dialog: "This male considers us a threat. We will not contest."

"Yeah, no contest," Dad muttered as the shuttle lifted off. It set us down a comfortable distance away on the far shore.

Day 3: Letter from Neesha to Landra

No entries yesterday. You can't write much when you're hugging a wet tree and your teeth are chattering.

The day started out real quiet—well, except for the pterosaurs squalling at one another on the beach. We all bailed out of the shuttle early to watch this neat herd of stegosaurs having breakfast in a stand of evergreens and cycads. They grunt like Gross Gary (remember him from astrometrics!?) when they rear up on their hind legs to reach a high branch. We didn't even notice that the sky was getting pretty dark in the southwest.

Then the ground shook. The stegs sniffed the air and started to move away. At first Mom thought it was an earthquake, but Dad pointed to a cloud of dust. "Stampede," he said, looking around kind of nervously. I knew we were a long way from the shuttle.

"We have to get up high," Dad said. Somehow, we all climbed this huge pine. Lizards, bugs, whatever—I knocked them all out of my way. No way did I want to be a stain on the foot of one of those sauropods.

It was a stampede all right, one that was being chased by a flood. Rain began to fall, and the wind slapped it in our faces. Lightning knocked down a tree a football field away. It seemed like the end of the world—with no ark in

Brachiosaurus:

Twenty-two feet high at the shoulder

Weight: ninety tons

Elephant:

Eleven feet high at the shoulder

Weight: six tons

Although *Brachiosaurus* was only twice as high at the shoulder as an elephant, it was about fifteen times heavier, with thicker legs relative to trunk size.

sight and the most bizarre parade of animals ever. We saw more stegosaurs, birdlike things with teeth and wing claws, ornithopods, crocodiles, turtles, and, of course, the sauropods—at least half a dozen different kinds. You could see the panic in their eyes when one of their big heads came close to our tree, but even with the floodwaters swirling all around them they seemed to move slow and dignified. Sometimes one of them would tip over in the water, thrashing its neck and tail. As big as they were, the sauropods were still no match for the water.

This morning the shuttle found us and landed nearby. The floodwaters left branches, downed trees, and dinosaur bodies everywhere. The shuttle's bug-bots hovered around us like nervous bees while we climbed down the tree. After that, everybody decided the intelligence that runs the ship is pretty nice to have around. We started calling him—it seems like a him, anyway—the Caretaker.

Miss ya.

—Neesha

I told Neesha not to eat those cycad salads. Now look at her!
—Jon

FOR 21ST-CENTURY EXPLORERS ...

Nathan Myhrvold of Microsoft research and Philip J. Currie of the Royal Tyrrell Museum in Alberta, Canada, studied the mechanics of sauropod tails with a commercial software program called Working Model. Their simulations indicate that the tip of an *Apatosaurus's* tail, when flicked, would reach a velocity of 540 meters per second—well above the speed of sound (350 meters per second). List some ways sauropods may have used their long tails. How might you test your ideas?

Dinosaurs were the largest land animals known. What are the limits to the size of a land animal? The diameter of the legs of an animal increase in proportion to its weight (which is also proportional to the volume of the animal's body). Use the graph on the next page, which plots circumference of an animal's leg bones versus body weight, and estimate answers to the following questions: If an animal weighs 100 pounds, what is the approximate circumference of its femur (upper leg bone*)? If you find a femur that is just under 40 inches in circumference, approximately how much did the animal weigh?** At a weight of approximately 140 tons (280,000 pounds), an animal's legs would be so wide that they would touch—and the animal couldn't walk!

**What did the *Troödon* say to the first mammals in its neighborhood?
The *Troödon* said:**

— — — — —   — — — — —   — — —   — — — — — —.

To solve this word puzzle, first group all the dinosaurs in the paragraph below into the geologic period in which they lived. For the purposes of this puzzle, assume the following: All prosauropods and coelurosaurs lived in the Triassic; all sauropods, Archeopteryx-like birds, stegosaurs, and allosaurs lived in the Jurassic; all hadrosaurs, ankylosaurs, and ceratopsians lived in the Cretaceous. Other dinosaurs are either mentioned in the text or can be looked up in a dinosaur reference.

After the dinosaurs are organized by geologic period, use the the first letter of their names to solve the word scramble. There will be one word from the Triassic group, two words from the Jurassic, and one word from the Cretaceous. Good luck!

Notoceratops (a ceratopsian), **R**hoetosaurus (a sauropod), **O**rnitholestes, **C**amarasaurus, **S**pondylosoma (a prosauropod), **R**egnosaurus (an ankylosaur), **P**lacerias, **E**dmontosaurus, **E**uskelosaurus (a prosauropod from South Africa), **A**vipes (a coelurosaur), **M**amenchisaurus, **L**ufengosaurus (a prosauropod from China), **O**smosaurus (a relative of Stegosaurus), **E**ucnemisaurus (a prosauropod from South Africa), **E**panterias (a type of Allosaur), **F**eathered dinosaurs (like *Archaeopteryx*), **D**yplosaurus (an ankylosaur), **I**guanodon, **N**ipponosaurus (a hadrosaur).

Answer: Please come for dinner.

* = Approximately 4 feet
** = 10 tons

REFERENCES

Czerkas, Sylvia J., and Stephen A. Czerkas. *Dinosaurs: A Global View.* New York: Mallard Press, 1991.

Czerkas, Sylvia J., and Everett C. Olson, eds. *Dinosaurs Past and Present.* Vol. 2. Seattle and London: Natural History Museum of Los Angeles County in association with the University of Washington Press, 1987.

De Courten, Frank. *Dinosaurs of Utah.* Salt Lake City: University of Utah Press, 1998.

Gillette, David D. *Seismosaurus: The Earth Shaker.* New York: Columbia University Press, 1994.

Gould, Stephen J., ed. *The Book of Life: An Illustrated History of the Evolution of Life on Earth.* New York: W. W. Norton, 1993. A very readable, adult reference with lots of great artwork.

Untermann, G. E., and B. R. Untermann. *A Popular Guide to the Geology of Dinosaur National Monument.* Dinosaur National Monument, UT: Dinosaur Nature Association, 1969.

Wilford, John Noble. *The Riddle of the Dinosaur.* New York: Alfred A. Knopf, 1985.

Earl Douglass

RESOURCES AND MAPS

In 1909, Earl Douglass went in search of a dinosaur "as big as a barn" so Andrew Carnegie would have an impressive museum exhibit. Douglass had a pretty good idea where to look: in northeastern Utah, where Jurassic-age rocks fanned out in the colorful Morrison Formation. Some of the first North American dinosaurs were found in the same formation near Denver in 1877.

Douglass was rewarded with the big discovery he was seeking: the most complete skeleton of *Apatosaurus* (formerly called *Brontosaurus*) ever found. He discovered a series of its tail vertebrae initially, after which he built a small cabin and moved his family to the site. Douglass spent the next fifteen years recovering and shipping the remains of a dozen species of dinosaurs, including *Stegosaurus, Allosaurus, Laosaurus, Camptosaurus,* and a young *Camarasaurus.*

Later, in his diary, Douglass wrote: "I hope that the Government, for the benefit of science and the people, will uncover a large area, leave the bones and skeletons in relief and house them in. It would make one of the most astounding and instructive sights imaginable."[2] Douglass's hope became

[2]Wilford, John Noble. *The Riddle of the Dinosaur.* New York: Alfred A. Knopf, 1985: 123.

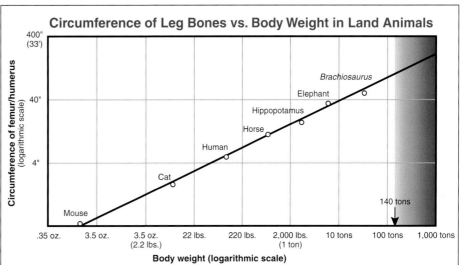

Circumference of Leg Bones vs. Body Weight in Land Animals

The chart shows that leg bone circumference (a linear measure) is directly proportional to weight (a cubic measure). Double the length of a 2-foot cube and its volume increases eight times. Bone circumferences can't increase fast enough to accommodate body weight. Eventually an animal's legs would have to be so thick that they would touch and the animal couldn't move! That limit is believed to be about 140 tons.

Body weights of dinosaurs can be estimated by making careful scale models and suspending them in water. The amount of water displaced equals their volume. Volume is directly proportional to weight. But what does a liter of dinosaur weigh? Living animals can vary from 1 pound per liter to .7 pound per liter depending on such things as how much air space is in their bones.

Dinosaur National Monument

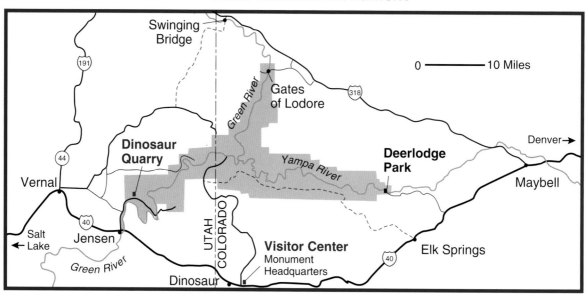

a reality. Dinosaur National Monument is headquartered near Vernal, Utah, and extends into the canyon country of northwestern Colorado. For more information contact:

Dinosaur National Monument
P.O. Box 128
Jensen, UT 84035
Phone: (801) 789-2115

Another site of interest in Utah is the Cleveland-Lloyd Dinosaur Quarry, a working quarry with tours and a visitor center. Most of the remains are of *Allosaurus*, which lived near the shore of a shallow lake near present day Price, Utah, 150 million years ago. For more information contact:

Cleveland-Lloyd Dinosaur Quarry
P.O. Drawer A.B.
Price, UT 84501
Phone: (801) 637-4584

Also in Price, Utah, is the Prehistoric Museum. It contains much of the material excavated from the Cleveland-Lloyd Dinosaur Quarry (see above). Visit or contact the museum at:

Prehistoric Museum
College of Eastern Utah
155 E. Main
Price, UT 84501
Phone: (435) 637-5060 or (800) 817-9949
Website: www.ceu.edu/museum/default.htm

THE JURASSIC WORLD

One Coelophysis cocked its head near
a big log, as if it heard something.
                    —Jon

Dinosaur Dawn

Jump 6: Triassic, 225 million years B.P.

Day 1: Entry by Jon Olifee

We landed before dawn again, so we had about an hour before the sun came up, but I couldn't sleep. I wandered out to the control room and Dad was already up trying to figure out from a whiz-bot how much longer our time jumps would go on. While they thoroughly confused each other, I watched some crow-sized pterosaurs through the viewscreens. They looked like they were dressed for Halloween. The most common kind had gargoylish eyes, a really long tail, and a snout with sharp, crooked teeth. One of them was perched in the lower branch of a huge evergreen that towered over a fern-fringed pond. It sat there for a while, slowly flexing its wing claws and staring at the surface of the water, and then, in a flash, swooped down, snatched some little fish, and flew off.

Once in a while we saw some creatures gliding from tree to tree. We finally got a good look when one of them crash-landed in a clearing near the pond. It was a lizard with wings called Icarosaurus, and its ribs formed the struts of its wings! I didn't have long to look, though. A twenty-foot-long phytosaur--that's what Mom called it later--lurched out of the undergrowth and crunched the lizard with one snap of its long jaws. About then, Dad came over and we both decided we were ready for breakfast.

Day 2: Entry by Neesha Olifee

My stomach is dancing and it's not from watching Dad and Jon eat. Most of the animals here are creepy. They look like a snake's first cousin. And the plants look goofy too. On the last jump I figured things seemed weird because there wasn't any grass anywhere,[1] but here it's even worse. The evergreens bush out at the top like spiky mushroom caps, lots of smaller trees look like overgrown ferns, and all the wet places are surrounded by overgrown horse-tails with ridged and jointed stems the size of telephone poles.

---

[1] Flowering plants first appeared about 100 million years ago. Grass evolved only 10 million years ago, during the Miocene epoch.

On a walk this afternoon we saw a herd of ox-sized animals called *Placerias* that weren't quite as lizardish as some things. They munched on ferns with their big, beaklike jaws and rooted in the dirt with funny-looking tusks. They snorted and looked at us with beady little eyes when we got too close. Some lizards with horns and spikes on their backs[2] pulled apart dead logs looking for insects. The heat and humidity finally drove us back to the shuttle for an early dinner.

Dad went fishing and came up with this lobe-finned beauty called a Coelocanth. People thought these were extinct until the 20th century, when some were found near Madagascar and in eastern Asia.
   --Jon

Day 3: Entry by Jon Olifee

Dinosaurs have chased us, nearly stomped us, and, in general, yellowed our underwear during each of the last three jumps. We've seen 160 million years' worth of dinos! Today we saw some of the first ones to evolve. There are small versions of sauropods called prosauropods, some critters that reminded me of hadrosaurs, and quick little theropods that zip through the forest undergrowth. We all decided we wanted to get a better look at those.

Mom suggested we set up a blind to hide ourselves by stacking a bunch of log-sized jointed plant stems. The result was kind of a green cabin with no roof. We got up early, snatched breakfast from the grease trough, and got situated inside the blind while it was still gray and foggy outside. Strange chirps, grunts, and growls from the forest kept even Neesha pretty quiet. She stayed near Dad and the sonic gun.

I was zoning out a little, thinking of the nice soft bunk webbing in the shuttle, when four six-foot-long Coelophysis appeared out of nowhere. They trotted on their hind legs like other theropods, pausing once in a while to sniff the air and look around. We all held our breath.

One Coelophysis cocked its head near a big log, as if it heard something. The others froze. Finally, the first one jabbed quickly with one forelimb claw and brought some wriggling thing to its mouth. About then the sun broke through the morning fog and we could see that the dino's breakfast was something small and furry. It didn't squiggle long. Dad popped off the sonic gun and the dinos scattered. I was glad. I was feeling a little small and furry myself.

Placerias out for a stroll.

[2] Perhaps *Desmatosuchus*.

FOR 21ST-CENTURY EXPLORERS ...

Before 1947 the little dinosaur *Coelophysis* was known from only a few stray bones. In that year Edwin H. Colbert found the mass grave of hundreds of these predators at Ghost Ranch, New Mexico. The excavation and preparation of these fossils have taken many years, but scientists have learned much about *Coelophysis* and its world through the methods of taphonomy—the study of what happens to creatures after they die but before they become fossils. Look at the diagram on the next page of the actual quarry and review the following paleontologists' chart of evidence and conclusions.

Evidence	Conclusions
Dinosaurs were buried in a broad, U-shaped expanse of siltstone.	The dinosaurs lived near a stream that sometimes flooded.
Lungfish burrows were found in some layers.	Like modern-day lungfish, the dinosaurs probably lived in a subtropical climate with wet and dry seasons.
The *Coelophysis* skeletons were piled up in a "body jam."	The bodies were probably piled up by floodwaters.
One layer (F) had the most bones, and 25 percent of the skeletons were still hooked together with little evidence of weathering.	This was the "kill layer," and the bodies must have been covered by sediment fairly quickly.
The bones had no tooth marks, punctures, cracks, or chewed-off ends.	Predators and scavengers didn't get to the animals.
The necks of the dinosaurs were bent back over their bodies, and layer F had mud cracks. Bones were scattered in layers above F.	The corpses dried out and their neck tendons contracted before burial. The original burial was later disturbed.
Small depressions were found in an area of irregular contact between layers H and J.	Animals later trampled the ground above the burial.
Bones of a young *Coelophysis* were found in the stomach area of an adult of the same species.	*Coelophysis* were sometimes cannibals!

What are some things that could have disturbed bones after burial (for example: floods, compaction of sediments, plant root growth, animals disturbing older sediments, earth movements)? What happened to hundreds of these early dinosaurs 225 million years ago? Why were so many predators in the same place at the same time? After more than forty years of study, scientists still haven't solved the entire mystery.

REFERENCES

Colbert, Edwin H. *The Great Dinosaur Hunters and Their Discoveries.* New York: Dover Publications, 1984. Reprint of *Men and Dinosaurs: The Search in Field and Laboratory,* New York: E. P. Dutton, 1968.

———. *The Little Dinosaurs of Ghost Ranch.* New York: Columbia University Press, 1995.

Gilette, David D. "The Age of Transition: Coelophysis and the Late Triassic Chinle Fauna." In Sylvia J. Czerkas and Everett C. Olson, eds. *Dinosaurs Past and Present.* Vol. 1. Seattle and London: Natural History Museum of Los Angeles County in association with the University of Washington Press, 1987.

Gore, Rick. "Extinctions." *National Geographic* 185, no. 6 (June 1989): 680–688.

Lubick, George M. *Petrified Forest National Park.* Tucson: University of Arizona Press, 1996.

RESOURCES AND MAPS

The little fish-eating pterosaur and the gliding lizard the Olifees watched lived in or near a forest of conifers related to modern-day Norfolk pines and monkey puzzle trees. These trees grew eighty to one hundred feet tall and about fifteen feet apart. Their tops bushed out and would have shaded the forest floor so that few other trees could live there, much like modern-day redwood forests. Tree ferns and cycads made up much of the understory. In

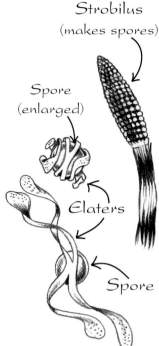

Equisetum (horsetail)

Strobilus (makes spores)

Spore (enlarged)

Elaters

Spore

Elaters get wet, expand, and push spores out.

Solving the Mysteries of the Ghost Ranch Fossils

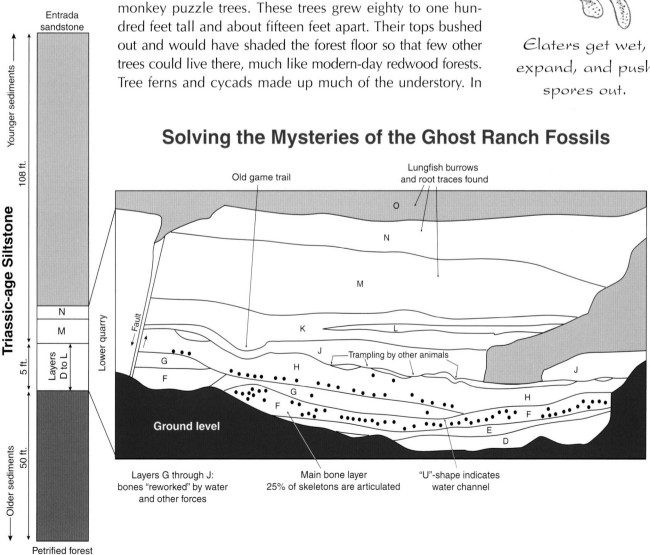

wetter areas horsetail-like trees with ridged and jointed trunks grew in thick bunches and sheltered alligator-like phytosaurs that sometimes reached lengths of twenty to thirty feet.

The very first dinosaurs also roamed these forests—small theropods like *Coelophysis*, miniature versions of Jurassic-age sauropods called prosauropods, and plant-eating fabrosaurs that would give rise to the hadrosaurs and other ornithischian dinosaurs. They shared their world with a tyrannosaur-like reptile called *Postosuchus*, spiny-backed plant-eaters called aetosaurs, and some of the first mammals—shrewlike animals that the meat-eaters probably considered tasty snacks.

You can drive through the remains of one of these Triassic-age forests at Petrified Forest National Park in Arizona, where huge tree trunks, logs, and occasional stumps have been turned into colorful hunks of jasper and chalcedony over a period of 225 million years. Visit stops called Blue Mesa, Jasper Forest, Agate Bridge, and Crystal Forest and see how time, wind, and water have preserved this glimpse into the distant past.

> Petrified Forest National Park
> 6618 Petrified Forest Rd.
> Holbrook, AZ 84028
> Phone: (520) 524-6822 (for the district ranger)

Park websites: www.nps.gov/pefo or
    www.2.nature.mps.gov/grd/parks/pefo
Commercial websites: www.petrified.forest.national-park.com or
    www.geocities/chinle_formation

Also in Arizona, check out:

> Museum of Northern Arizona
> 3101 N. Fort Valley Rd.
> Flagstaff, AZ 86001
> Phone: (520) 774-5213
> Website: www.musnaz.org

In New Mexico, check out the Ghost Ranch Conference Center, which has a display of more than a hundred *Coelophysis* skeletons, and the New Mexico Museum of Natural History.

> Ghost Ranch Conference Center
> HC 77 Box 11
> Abiquiu, NM 87501
> Phone: (505) 685-4333

> New Mexico Museum of Natural History
> 1801 Mountain Rd. N.W.
> Albuquerque, NM 87104
> Phone: (505) 841-2802

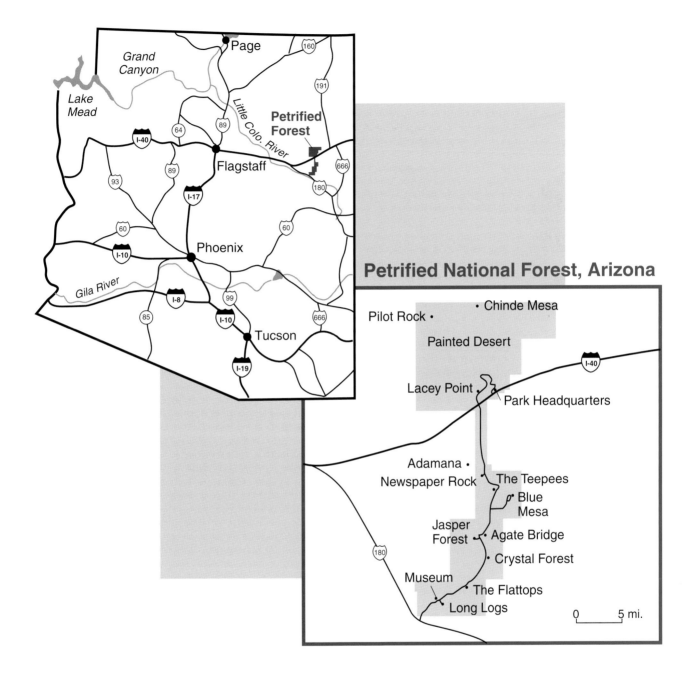

Petrified National Forest, Arizona

THE TRIASSIC WORLD

Miss "I love bugs" found what she thought was a log.
—Jon

Storm in Green Forest

Jump 7: Carboniferous (late Pennsylvanian), 295 million years B.P.

Day 1: Entry by Neesha Olifee

We left the shuttle as soon as the sun was up. The cool sand squished between my toes. Real zifty shells lay all around, and I started picking them up—that is, before I saw the forest up by the cliffs. Too weird. The trees looked like huge, green poles—some had kinda feathery tops and others looked like bottle brushes! Didn't have long to look, though, 'cause something BIG whirred past my ear and I dived for the ground.

"Afraid of dragonflies?" Jon laughed as I got up. I glared at him, spitting sand. That thing was as big as a hawk! Pretty soon another one chased after the first and grabbed it by its rear end. The second one's tail looped under the first's, and they flew around near Jon like a black-and-blue ring. They were mating. I'd seen dragonflies do that in the marsh near home. Jon's face turned red. I smiled at him. "Afraid of dragonflies having sex?" I asked.

We stayed on the beach the rest of the day. We saw a six-foot-long thing washed up on shore that looked like a cross between a scorpion and a crayfish. Dad said it was a eurypterid. With its big eyes and bigger claws it looked like something that used to have an attitude. Now it was bug bait.

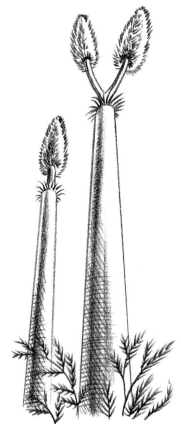

Poster plant for Tidy Bowl if I ever saw one.

—Jon

Strobilus

Stem

Leaf

Root

Tuber

A lycopod seedling (club moss) still around in 21st century!

Day 2: Entry by Jon Olifee

All four of us hiked over to "Green Forest." A few bug-bots flew along too. We followed a meandering stream through marshy wetlands. Bugs buzzed all over the place, and there were salamander-like things the size of small gators (with teeth to match!) that scurried into the water as we passed. At first it looked like it was going to be a nice, sunny day like yesterday. In fact, we saw a bunch of pelycosaurs with their spinal fins spread way out, sunning themselves on the ridge.

The funniest thing happened when we stopped for a snack. Neesha found what she thought was a log, but when she plopped herself down on it, it starting moving. She yelped and jumped up like a boulder had just landed on the far side of her teeter-totter. The "log" was actually a brownish-black-colored millipede six feet long and a foot wide. It crawled off on its bazillion legs and disappeared into a crack in the limestone. Seems Miss "I love bugs" finally met her match.

After lunch the bug-bots seemed agitated and flew up and spiraled over our heads. We noticed it was getting cloudy in the west and Dad said we better be sure to head back well before dark.

It seemed like we hiked forever among giant trees with scaly trunks--lycopods, they're called. We pushed our way through clumps of seed ferns and bunches of overgrown horse-tails like the ones on the last jump. Lots of lizards scooted up tree trunks and peeked at us from behind the branches. Neesha thought they were cute.

The wind came up all at once. It moaned through what passed for pine trees on the dry ridgelines. Some of the

Sun-worshiping pelycosaurs

lycopods swayed and creaked around us. Dad said that we should head back.

We walked pretty fast at first, but when it started to rain we had to slow down on the rocky parts. Neesha almost tripped over a spider the size of a dinner plate. I pulled her back just as it reared up on its hind legs and showed its shiny green fangs.

A gust of wind caught a tree just ahead of us. It leaned way over and we heard a loud crack as its roots pulled up out of the mucky soil. It fell like Goliath cut off at the knees and crashed into the stream, throwing water and mud everywhere. Mom pointed to a cave not far away in the cliffs, and we managed to stumble our way there without too many bruises.

Neesha really likes brachiopod shells!

—Jon

Day 2: Letter from Neesha to Landra

The night in the cave was cold and wet. We didn't sleep much. The forest—and the bug-bots, for that matter—made too many strange sounds. Next day was sunny, but trees were down everywhere, like some giant forgot his "pick-up-sticks."

Before we left the forest, I found one of those cute lizards stuck inside a rotting tree stump. He was half buried in mud and looked at me as if he wanted to say, "I'm too tired to run."

He zipped away, though, when I lifted him out and set him down. Jon said maybe I changed history by doing that. Maybe so, I don't know. I think even a lizard needs a break now and then. I bet you do too. Hope to see you soon.

—Neesha

Seed pod

Calamites stem

Seed fern (Neuropteris)

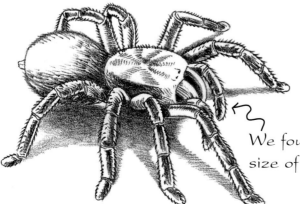

We found a tarantula the size of a dinner plate.

FOR 21ST CENTURY EXPLORERS ...

Lycopods and horsetails are the only modern-day descendants of the ancient Carboniferous-age forests. They reproduce by spores rather than seeds. Mosses are more common spore-bearing plants that grow in damp spots in woodlands. Their spores are borne in brownish spore cases on tall stalks called sporangia. Try growing a moss culture of your own. Find a patch of moss with sporangia in a damp, woodland area. Collect a small handful of spore cases. Put them in a blender with one cup of milk and blend thoroughly. Pour the mixture into a one-quart container and fill it with more milk. Pour this "moss milk" into crevices between bricks or stones. The milk provides nourishment, but you must also keep the area watered. The growing moss will look like green fuzz.

To better understand how prehistoric fish may have developed into amphibians, observe the development of frogs. Collect frog eggs from nearby wetlands. They look like raisins, embedded in a clear jelly—often attached to the stems of water plants. Have an adult help you create a balanced aquarium to serve as a home to the frogs for a few weeks. Monitor the eggs as they hatch and develop into tadpoles. Eventually, the tadpoles will absorb their tails and gills and develop legs. Once the tadpoles have developed into young frogs, return them to the area where you collected the eggs.

Cockroaches have changed little since the Carboniferous period. Visit a pet store and see if they carry Madagascar hissing cockroaches. At two and a half inches in length, the Madagascar variety are about the same size as some of their primitive, Carboniferous-age relatives. Why do you think cockroaches have been such successful survivors?

REFERENCES

Dixon, Dougal, Barry Cox, R.J.G Savage, and Brian Gardiner. *The Macmillan Illustrated Encyclopedia of Dinosaurs and Prehistoric Animals.* New York: Macmillan Publishing, 1988.

Gould, Stephen J., ed. *The Book of Life: An Illustrated History of the Evolution of Life on Earth.* New York: W. W. Norton, 1993. A very readable, adult reference with lots of great artwork.

Johnson, Kirk R., and Richard K. Stucky. *Prehistoric Journey.* Boulder, CO: Roberts Rinehart Publishers, 1995. Produced in conjunction with a recently new permanent exhibit at the Denver Museum of Natural History.

Palmer, Douglas. *Atlas of the Prehistoric World.* New York: Discovery Books, 1999.

Stanley, Stephen M. *Earth and Life Through Time.* New York: W. H. Freeman, 1986. Excellent textbook that looks at geology with a paleontologist's eye.

Stein, Sara. *The Evolution Book.* New York: Workman Publishing, 1986. Lots of engaging student activities for young readers.

RESOURCES AND MAPS

The "Green Forest" explored by the Olifees may have been located in what is now present-day eastern Kansas. The small farming community of Hamilton, Kansas, rests on layered limestone deposited by an ancient sea that existed there 295 million years ago, during the Carboniferous period. On land, odd-looking forests of lycopods—some with quilt-barked stems and others with bottle-brush tops—grew tall and thick and sheltered a host of giant insects, amphibians, and lizards. The trees were probably entirely green because they didn't have the specialized tissue of modern-day trees that transports starch from leaves and minerals from roots to all parts of the plant.

One of the best ways to see this world is to visit the Denver Museum of Nature and Science's Prehistoric Journey exhibit. Fossils from Hamilton make up part of the exhibit. If you can't visit the museum, check out their website: www.dmns.org. You can also buy a book called *Prehistoric Journey* (written by Kirk Johnson and Richard Stucky—see the "References" section on pg. 52), which beautifully describes and illustrates the exhibit. The museum is located at: 2001 Colorado Blvd., Denver, CO 80205. Phone: (303) 370-6357.

Carboniferous-age fossils (often associated with coal deposits) occur in many places, including Pennsylvania, Mississippi, Illinois, Kentucky, West Virginia, Nova Scotia, England, France, Germany, Poland, and Russia. See if you can find a site in your area.

Nosy lizard checking out a Lepidodendron tree trunk. Tasty insects hide in there.

Sporangium

Typical moss plant

Area for Carboniferous-age Fossils in Eastern Kansas

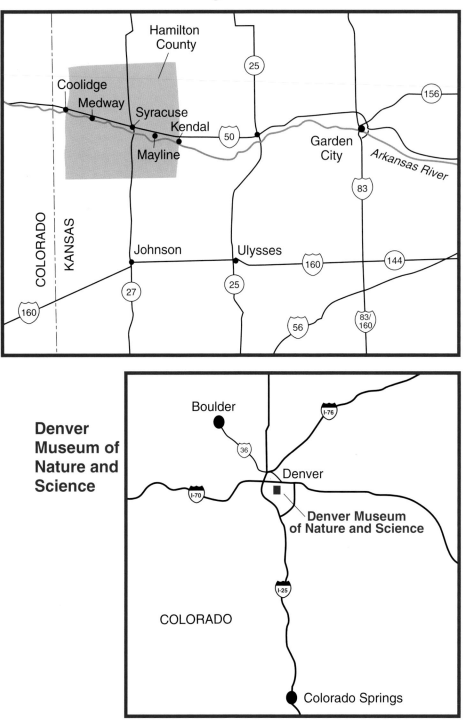

THE CARBONIFEROUS WORLD

We looked up and saw a dark, torpedo-shaped
creature blocking out the light from the sun.
—Neesha

Animalocaris
and the Butterflies of the Sea

Jump 8: Middle Cambrian, 525 million years B.P.

Day 1: Entry by Jon Olifee

Neesha and I made the discovery of the day: We climbed up this pile of rocks at low tide looking for a little bit of shade and a spot to eat our snacks from the grease trough. Even with the oxy-booster shot,[1] I was breathing hard and sweat kept trickling into my eyes. I lathered on some more sunscreen and wiped the sweat from under my hat brim. I turned to hand Neesha the lotion, but she wasn't there.

"Up here!" I heard her yell from above. When I looked up, she waved from the top of the ridge. "Stay there, grub," I said, "before you break your neck." I scrambled up a boulder pile to reach her side. She pointed out Mom and Dad a few hundred yards down the beach, but I saw something else much closer, just below us. "Wow," I said. Neesha turned to look, then took a step closer to me. "What is that?" she asked.

"One monster-sized trilobite," I said. It lay in a bathtub-sized tide pool and must have been three feet long. It fluttered its legs now and then and twitched its antennae—which were half as long as its body. Its large, faceted eyes shimmered with rainbow colors in the bright sunlight.

Later, when Dad came up to draw a picture of the trilobite, we saw the feathery gills attached to each walking leg. Neesha liked its shell: lumpy, spiny, and the color of butterscotch with black and rust-colored stripes. She called him Tiger. I remember seeing fossil trilobites in school. They

---

[1] The Olifees found oxygen levels to be less than the modern norm. Thus ozone levels in the upper atmosphere were also lower.

"Tiger"! Isn't he a beaut!
—Neesha

were always the same dull gray or brown color as the rock. Too bad colors don't fossilize because this guy would have won a prize!

By the time we left, the tide was up near the base of the rock pile. Next morning Tiger was gone, back out to sea. I hope he found his way home all right. His home is a lot closer than ours.

Day 2: Entry by Neesha Olifee

The bug-bots made some underwater gear today, so we went reef diving! We saw all kinds of trilobites—must have been Tiger's cousins. Mom called them Butterflies of the Sea.[2] They fluttered around us—in every shape, size, and color—as we swam along the reef. Some seemed to be finding worms to eat near the flowery-looking coral animals. Others filtered smaller goodies out of the water. Dad said trilobites have to do all the jobs fish do in the oceans of our time.

On the ocean bottom, more trilobites crawled along in the mud, some raising clouds of dirt as they tried to dig in and hide from us. It made it hard to see anything. Mom got nervous. She said if the trilobites were afraid of something our size, that must mean there were some predators out there that we might want to watch out for ourselves.

Sure enough, not much later, swimming our way through a field of sea lilies,[3] we noticed that most of the trilobites had disappeared. Dad motioned us to be still. Not long after, a shadow passed over us. We looked up and saw a dark, torpedo-shaped creature blocking out the light from the sun. I got goosebumps.

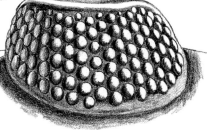

Trilobites had compound eyes long before insects did!

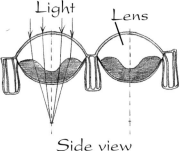

Light   Lens

Side view

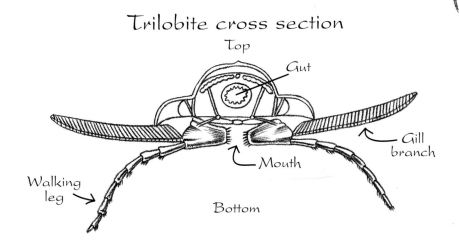

Trilobite cross section

Top

Gut

Gill branch

Mouth

Walking leg

Bottom

"Spiny"

---

[2] The paleontologist Percy Edward Raymond gave this nickname to trilobites in 1939.

[3] Animals related to starfish that hooked themselves to the ocean bottom with stalks.

Trilobites molt to get bigger.

Sea lily
(a crinoid)

Priapulid
worm

Dinomischus

Hyolithes

Dad called it *Animalocaris*, and it had a pair of tentacles hanging down from one end near a mouth that looked like a round hole ringed with a set of overlapping knives. It swam with flaps that rippled like broad, rubbery oars. It kind of coasted for a while, but suddenly made a swooping dive at the reef. A trilobite hung from underneath the shadow-beast for a moment, but pretty soon it just seemed to crumple and then disappeared into the round mouth. Only a few legs and a dark stain trailed the shadow-beast as it swam away. Yuk.

That night we made a campfire and pretended the edible white things from the grease trough were marshmallows. While Dad and Jon were trying to figure out constellations, a whiz-bot joined us and pointed in the general direction of the star Sirius. It said something like "Ten-or-ee home," then clammed up. I shivered. I remember falling asleep thinking that all those bright stars looked just like glittering trilobites dancing near a milky-colored reef.

REFERENCES

Thompson, Ida. *The Audubon Society Field Guide to North American Fossils.* New York: Alfred A. Knopf, 1982.

Fenton, Carroll Lane, and Mildred Adams. **The Fossil Book.** New York: Doubleday, 1989. Chapter 12 is all about trilobites.

"Index Trilobites of North America." Poster distributed by Paleo-arts Publications, division of Mid-land Scientific, 1157 Behnfeldt, Bryan, OH 43506.

Levi-Setti, Riccardo. **Trilobites.** 2nd ed. Chicago: University of Chicago Press, 1993. Advanced text, but lots of great photos.

Raham, R. Gary. "The Bugs that Aren't." **Highlights for Children,** April 1998.

————. **Dinosaurs in the Garden.** Medford, NJ: Plexus Publications, 1988. Chapter 9 is all about pill bugs.

————. "Time Traveling with Trilobites." **Highlights Plus Science Supplement to Highlights for Children,** January 1998.

FOR 21ST-CENTURY EXPLORERS ...

Trilobites flourished for 300 million years before becoming extinct in the "Great Dying" 250 million years ago. Living relatives that share some of their features include horseshoe crabs and the tiny garden crustaceans called pill bugs, or roly-polys.

Look for pill bugs under rocks or moist leaf litter near your home. When you disturb one, it rolls up into a ball. Many trilobites could do this as well. What purpose would this behavior serve?

Flip a pill bug over onto its back. It has thirteen pairs of legs. Trilobites usually had eighteen pairs or more, but with much variation. Each trilobite leg had an attached gill for breathing underwater. Crayfish and other water crustaceans have leg gills as well. A pill bug breathes with the help of two white, bean-shaped structures on its belly, near its rear end.

Trilobites lived so long and left so many fossils throughout the Paleozoic era that they are used as index fossils. Index fossils are fossils that are only found in certain layers of rock, so wherever those layers are found, anywhere in the world, scientists know they are similar in age. Find out which trilobites are index fossils for the following periods of Paleozoic time: Cambrian period, Ordovician period, Silurian period, Devonian period, Carboniferous period, and Permian period.

RESOURCES AND MAPS

Trilobites made Earth their home for 250 million years. Not only did the dead animals become fossils, but their cast-off shells became fossils as well. As a result, you can find fossil trilobites in many places worldwide.

Always get permission from landowners before fossil hunting. Local rock clubs often lead summer field trips to nearby rock, mineral, and fossil sites. Visit a local library or museum, or ask your science teacher, to learn more about such groups.

The inset map on p. 61, of western Utah, shows you how to get to a commercial digging quarry called U-Dig Fossils. They charge hourly or daily fees for digging fossils and provide some tools and assistance. Most of the land surrounding the quarry is owned either by the state or by the Bureau of Land Management. Check current federal and state regulations before fossil hunting on public lands.

Expect to work through hot, dry, dusty days—bring plenty of water. Nights are cool. Average elevation is 7,000 feet, and the ground tends to be rocky and gravely with scrubby plants and few trees. Roads are gravel once you leave U.S. Highway 50/6 and are in good shape unless it has rained hard recently. If you plan to camp overnight, bring your own wood for fires.

Bring rock hammers, chisels, and perhaps a pry bar. Wear a hat, and lather on the sunscreen. Sturdy boots will help protect your feet from sharp rocks and unexpected rattlesnakes.

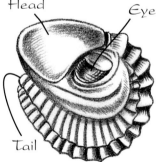

Rolled up trilobite
(Kainops invias)
Head   Eye
Tail

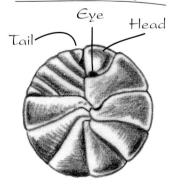

Rolled up pill bug
(Armadillidium Vulgare)
Tail   Eye   Head

For more information contact the quarry:
U-Dig Fossils
P.O. Box 1113
Delta, UT 84624
Phone: (801) 864-3638

For a good visual display of trilobites, obtain a copy of the poster "Index Trilobites of North America" (see the "References" section on p. 59).

Trilobite Tales, a newsletter published by the Western Interior Paleontological Society (WIPS) of Denver, has great information about all aspects of paleontology. WIPS also offers certification classes for paleontological techniques and great summer field trips. Contact WIPS at:
Western Interior Paleontological Society
P.O. Box 200011
Denver, CO 80220
Website: www.wipsppc.com

Some trilobite localities in the United States are:
Jersey County, Illinois (Edgewood Formation)
Cape Girardeau County, Missouri (Maquoketa Formation)
Cass County, Nebraska (Virgil Series)
Oneida County, New York (Trenton Group)
Orange County, New York (Niagara Series, Trilobite Ridge)
Clinton County, Ohio (Arnheim Formation)
Lucas County, Ohio (Silica Shale Formation)
Wayne County, Ohio (Cincinnati Group)
Carter County, Oklahoma (Bromide Formation)
York County, Pennsylvania (Kinzer Formation)
Millard County, Utah (Wheeler Formation)

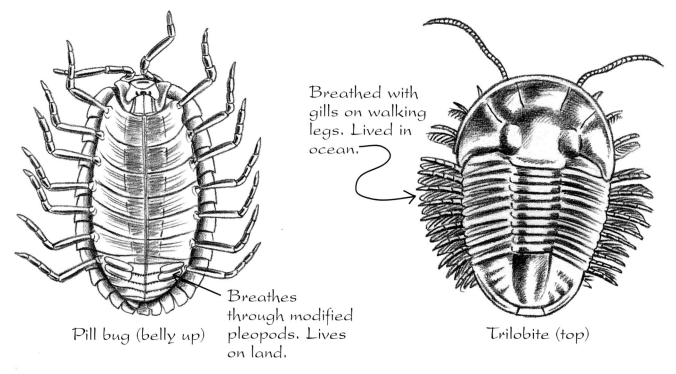

Breathed with gills on walking legs. Lived in ocean.

Breathes through modified pleopods. Lives on land.

Pill bug (belly up)

Trilobite (top)

U-Dig Fossils and the Trilobites of the Sevier Desert

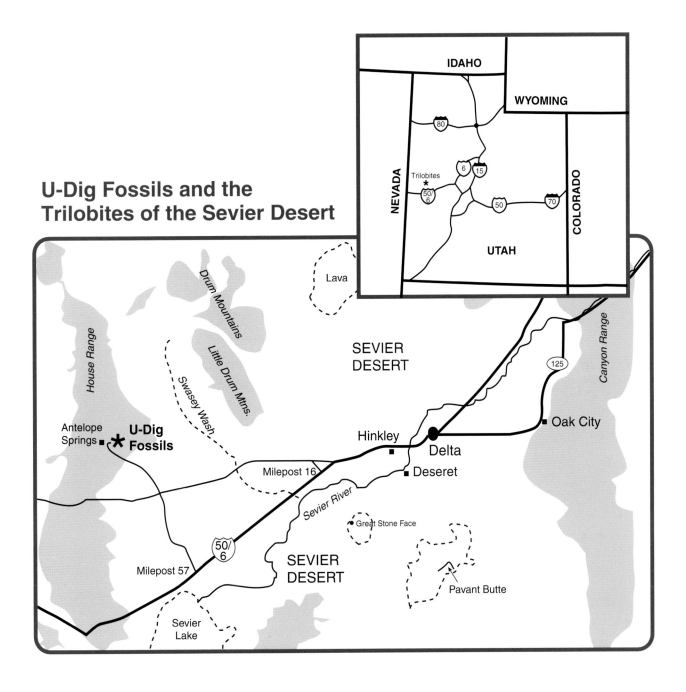

IDAHO

WYOMING

NEVADA

80

6 15

Trilobites
★
50/6

50

70

COLORADO

UTAH

Lava

SEVIER DESERT

Drum Mountains

Little Drum Mtns.

House Range

Swasey Wash

Canyon Range

125

Antelope Springs ■ ● ★ **U-Dig Fossils**

Hinkley ■

Delta ●

■ Oak City

Milepost 16

■ Deseret

Sevier River

Milepost 57

50/6

● Great Stone Face

SEVIER DESERT

Pavant Butte

Sevier Lake

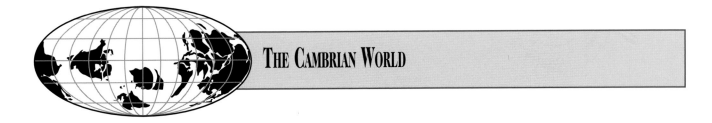

THE CAMBRIAN WORLD

Sometimes a volcano belched sooty columns of gray smoke, or a lake steamed like some witch's kettle.
                                    —Neesha

To What End?

Jump 9: Precambrian, 800 million years B.P.

Day 1: Entry by Neesha Olifee

As we got closer to Earth after our last jump, I held my breath til I thought I would faint. Snow at both poles! A few spots of light on the dark side of the terminator! If those were cities, I planned to eat chocolate for breakfast, lunch, and dinner. But through the thin clouds I could make out three odd-shaped continents clustered near the equator. The bright specks were some crummy volcanoes, not chocolate factories.

It got worse. As the shuttle flew low over one continent, miles and miles of bare rock and sand dunes seemed to stretch into forever. Sometimes a volcano belched sooty columns of gray smoke, or a lake steamed like some witch's kettle. But most mountains were snow-covered. Dad pointed out mountain glaciers even near the equator. Who or what could live down there? Who wanted to? Not me.

Day 1: Entry by Jon Olifee

We landed near some hot springs. Dad checked the ship's external readouts and things are livable outside, even if it does look like holograms of Mars Base. Oxygen levels are a little low, like living in Peru or something. Mom says microscopic ocean plants have been cranking out oxygen for a couple of billion years, but there are no land plants to help out.

I get cold just watching glaciers.
—Neesha

Carbon dioxide levels are lots less too. Dad says that's why there's so much snow in the mountains and at the poles: not many greenhouse gases.

Mom calls the hot springs "a rainbow of life in a vast desert." She gets that way sometimes. The pools are kind of pretty—streaks of yellow, orange, green, and purple stain the edges of the pools and the places the steam keeps hot and wet. Dad says the whole genetic future of the planet is trapped in tide pools like this, as well as in the oceans. All the major chemical pathways, like photosynthesis and respiration, have been worked out over the last several billion years. Everything else we've seen throughout time is just reshuffled DNA details. Maybe so, but I've nearly been eaten or stepped on by some scary-looking "details."

Day 2: Entry by Neesha Olifee

We'd just finished one of our grease-trough delights tonight when a whiz-bot whirred out of somewhere and said, "Greetings, Olifee family! Your language is fibrous and hard to chew, but I have done it! I will explain with the clearness of crystal why you have been my guests on this journey." Then the whizzer turned to me and said, "For you, Neesha, I can even explain in Pig Latin." Just what we needed—an alien stand-up comic.

Well, we did laugh a lot, but mostly the Caretaker made perfect sense: He was made several thousand years ago (measured from the time period we are in now) by a race called the Tenori—which roughly translates as "those who cherish." They found Earth, got homesick for their own planet, which got fried in a super-nova explosion generations before, and decided to build a time machine so that whatever intelligent life evolved here could

The Earth
with acne!
—Jon

appreciate all that had come before. Somehow, they felt pretty confident intelligent life would develop here and they also knew they wouldn't survive forever. Their "spirits were still bright," said the whiz-bot, "but their numbers were too small." They knew they would become extinct soon, just like the dinosaurs and Old Gimp, the sabertooth.

About then Mom came over and put her arm around my shoulder. "We've enjoyed our trip," she said to the whiz-bot, "but we don't belong here. It's not our time. We want to go home."

Yeah, tell 'em, Mom, I thought.

Day 3: Entry by Jon Olifee

The Caretaker said today he can get us home, but we have to sleep our way there in some kind of suspended-animation cylinders because the wormhole portal is strictly one-way. The cylinders look too much like coffins to me. Dad must not be too impressed, either, because he suggested we leave a kind of time pod behind containing the records we've been keeping. Mom agrees. She says the time pods will be our message-in-a-bottle to the future, letting people know how grand and complicated life has been on this old planet. She has faith in the Caretaker she says, but it's always a good idea to have a Plan B.

The Caretaker promises that the journey back to our own time will be both safe and exciting. He says he wants us to see some of Earth's "crisis points" so that we can appreciate both how tough and how delicate life on Earth can be. So I guess that means our suspended-animation cylinders will have some fancy alarm clocks to wake us up once in a while.

"Whiz-bot" in lecture mode.
Why do you suppose all teachers
look about the same?
—Neesha

Day 14: Letter from Neesha to Landra

This may be my last note to you. The fix-bots helped us put together some super-tough time pods with special, coded seals to make sure some Neanderthal doesn't pop them open early. We buried one pod with Jon's and my records and another with Dad's official logs. Our "sleep coffins" will be in another spot.

Don't worry, Landra, that's just a fun term. Even though the shuttle crashed near Fossil Lake, and the scrambled eggs we get in the grease trough taste like french toast, and the Caretaker talks lousy Pig Latin, he does seem pretty nice, and pretty smart too. I hope pretty smart is good enough to get us home.

We've seen great things the last couple of days—so much that neither Jon nor I have made any diary entries. Jon's been flop-jawed about how big the moon looks. Its closer to Earth than it will be in our time, you know. The hot springs are kind of beautiful if you don't mind the smell of rotten eggs. And we've been ocean-snorkeling in a cove that has fantastic, feathery creatures like none you've ever seen. Some look like sheets of jelly, others wave on stalks. You can't really tell if they're animals or plants. Dad's been wearing his pencils down to nubs drawing pictures.

I found a spot I bet you'd like as much as I do. My voice bounces off high rock walls and meets itself coming back. I can yell as loud as I want and there are no neighbors within millions of years to complain about it! Love you, Landra. See you in 800 million birthdays or so.

—Your best friend,

Neesha

REFERENCES

Edgar, Blake. "The Ultimate Missing Link." *Earth* 6, no. 5 (October 1997): 30–31.

Gould, James L., and Carol Grant. *Life at the Edge.* New York: W. H. Freeman, 1989.

Margulis, Lynn, and Dorion Sagan. *Microcosmos.* New York: Summit Books, 1986.

McMenamin, Mark A. S. *The Garden of Ediacara.* New York: Columbia University Press, 1998.

Mestel, Rosie. "Kimberella's Slippers." *Earth* 6, no. 5 (October 1997): 24–30.

Monastersky, Richard. "The Rise of Life on Earth." *National Geographic* 193, no. 3 (March 1998): 54–81.

Schopf, William J. *Major Events in the History of Life.* Boston: Jones & Bartlett Publishers, 1992.

Wright, Karen. "When Life Was Odd." *Discover* 18, no. 3 (March 1997): 52–61.

RESOURCES AND MAPS

Steaming pools with microscopic life very much like that the Olifees saw 800 million years ago can still be found today in places like Yellowstone National Park. "And behold!" exclaimed Joseph Meek in 1829, when he first saw the Yellowstone Valley. "The whole country beyond was smoking with vapor from boiling springs, and burning with gases issuing from small craters, each of which was emitting a sharp, whistling sound."[1] The rolling western landscape of pine trees, mountains, and wildflowers seems out of place near bubbling cauldrons of water that contain microorganisms that not only survive but happily thrive in water that is 190° F.

These creatures, called extremophiles because they live in conditions deadly for most life today, reflect a time billions of years ago when Earth was a hot and violent place. These microorganisms make a living turning iron and sulfur compounds into energy. When Earth cooled, and other, more efficient metabolic pathways produced caustic by-products such as oxygen, these creatures retreated to hot springs and deep ocean vents, where volcanic forces kept things warm and comfy. They were has-beens even 800 million years ago.

The new kids on the block then were feathery fronds, disks, and flattened blobs that looked a little like air mattresses. They had no heads or tails, no eyes or mouths, and no "systems" of any kind to process food or carry on life's functions. They lived on ocean bottoms and let ocean currents bring them food and carry away wastes. They are called the Ediacarans after the Australian Hills where many of their fossilized impressions are found. Scientists also study their remains in England, in Africa, and in the cliffs near the White Sea in northern Russia. Exactly what they looked like and how they lived are mysteries waiting to be solved. Were they a failed evolutionary experiment or our most distant relatives? It will be fun trying to find the answers to these and other questions.

[1] Hiram Martin Chittenden, *The Yellowstone National Park* (Norman: University of Oklahoma Press, 1964), 40.

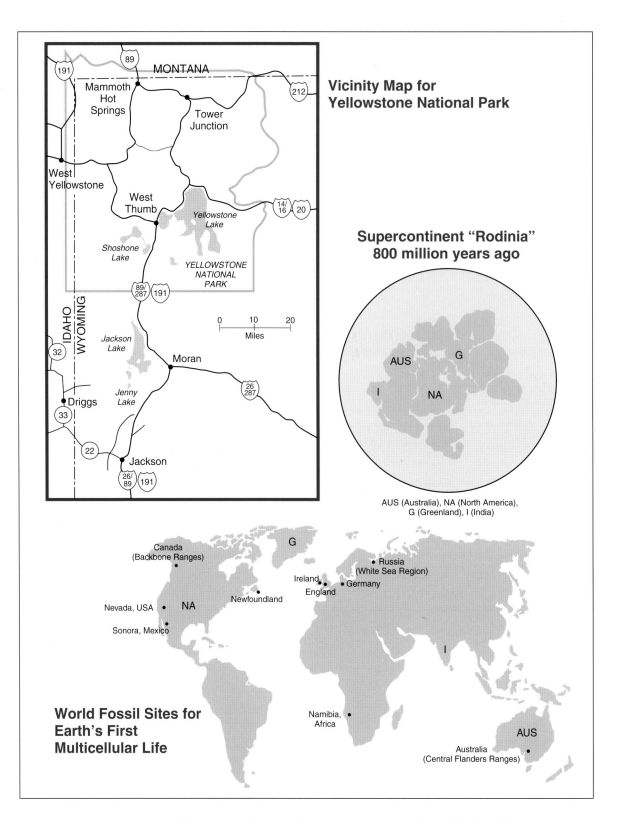

Vicinity Map for Yellowstone National Park

Supercontinent "Rodinia" 800 million years ago

AUS (Australia), NA (North America), G (Greenland), I (India)

World Fossil Sites for Earth's First Multicellular Life

For more information about Yellowstone, contact the park directly:

Yellowstone National Park

National Park Service

P.O. Box 168

Yellowstone National Park, WY 82190

Phone: (307) 344-7381

Website: www.yellowstone.org

An Overview
OF EARTH HISTORY AND THE OLIFEES' TRAVEL LOG

By Jon Olifee

TRANSCRIBER'S NOTE: Jon compiled the following information near the end of their journey, just before the family committed to "sleeping" back to their own time with the Caretaker. It nicely puts their travels in perspective relative to the history of life on Earth.

We're 800 million years away from home. It's hard to breathe outside and it looks as bare as the moon. "Pond scum" and some Ediacaran air-mattress animals are the only living things around besides us. The Caretaker has let me use the onboard computers to put together this overview of our trip. I'll put it in the time capsule with the diaries Neesha and I have been keeping.

Earth is 4.5 billion years old—the same age as the moon, meteors, and other parts of the solar system, all condensed from the same cloud of gas and dust.

Life got started about 3.5 billion years ago. We know this because scientists in our time found microfossils in some of Earth's oldest rocks. The earliest microbes used chemicals like methane and sulfur to make energy, and lived at pressures and temperatures that would have made toast of us. Then, somewhere around 3.2 billion years ago, some creatures that may have looked a lot like blue-green "pond scum" invented photosynthesis: take carbon dioxide and water, hook them to some chlorophyll molecules, zap with sunlight, and you get sugars and oxygen.

Between 2 and 2.2 billion years ago, Earth had its first pollution problem: too much oxygen. Oxygen reacts with everything—living and non-living. The old methane-sulfur bacteria went into hiding in deep mud and rocks, and other life-forms built defenses. Meanwhile, lots of rock rusted, forming banded iron "red beds."

From there on the story of life has been a story of disaster and recovery. That's how geologists can divide up geologic time in the first place. Every time a disaster happened, some things died and other things changed, carried on, and sometimes left their bones and shells behind. Five major disasters happened since large fossils started to form 590 million years ago. The biggest disaster, 250 million years ago, nearly wiped the planet clean. The second biggest disaster, 65 million years ago, blew away the dinosaurs. After that, tiny shrewlike mammals had the world to themselves. Like Mom said, "The once weak and sometimes meek inherited the Earth."

The next six pages show our time jumps. Each page represents about 100 million years. I added some of Dad's drawings from each jump. We had some real mind-popping adventures. The Caretaker says we'll have some more on the way back—and that's fine: I'm ready. But it's sure going to feel good to see my old friends again. And the first thing I'm going to do is have one of them find a chocolate bar for Neesha and another find me the largest bowl of ice cream on the planet!

Left: Two primitive primates peer from an Eocene forest while *Diatryma* looks on from behind.

Below: An ornithomimid mother guards her nest.

**Jump #2:
Jungle
Disaster**

**Jump #1:
Teratorns
& Tar Pits**

Old Gimp, the sabre-toothed cat, looks through the tusks of a mammoth trapped some time ago in a tar pit. A Teratorn flies overhead looking for fresher victims.

Mega-extinction #2 (rated in order of severity): Dinosaurs get zapped. Reasons: Giant inland sea drains; lots of volcanoes in India; giant asteroid whacks future northern Mexico.

**Jump #3:
Mother
Trouble**

Time in millions of years

65

Mammals take over niches left after dinosaurs die out. Grasses outcompete other plants in disturbed habitats. Other angiosperms diversify. Human-like primates develop over the last million years of the period. Modern humans appear about 100,000 years ago.

Flowering plants begin to show dominance on land. The Western Interior Seaway divides North America into western and eastern halves.

CENOZOIC

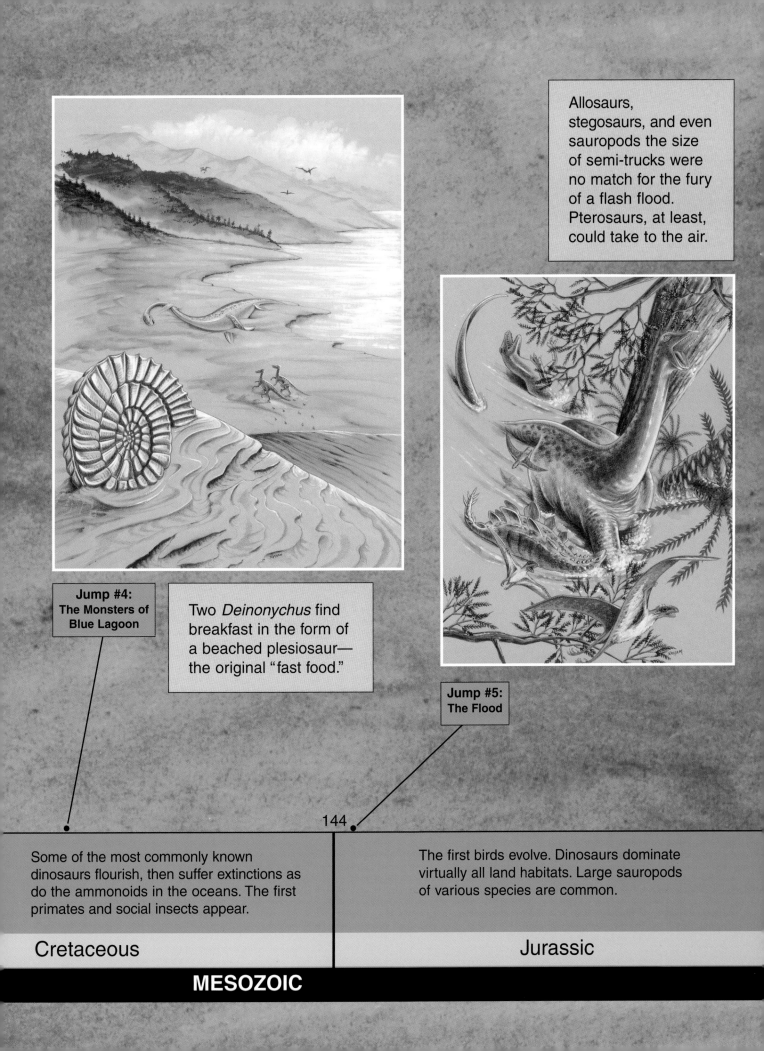

Allosaurs, stegosaurs, and even sauropods the size of semi-trucks were no match for the fury of a flash flood. Pterosaurs, at least, could take to the air.

Jump #4:
The Monsters of Blue Lagoon

Two *Deinonychus* find breakfast in the form of a beached plesiosaur— the original "fast food."

Jump #5:
The Flood

144

Some of the most commonly known dinosaurs flourish, then suffer extinctions as do the ammonoids in the oceans. The first primates and social insects appear.

The first birds evolve. Dinosaurs dominate virtually all land habitats. Large sauropods of various species are common.

Cretaceous

Jurassic

MESOZOIC

Compsognathus, a dinosaur from Jurassic-age Germany, had a skeletal structure very similar to the primitive birds *(Archeopteryx)* that it's chasing.

Two *Coelophysis* cast nervous glances at *Postosuchus,* a large predatory reptile sharing their Triassic forest.

Jump #6: Dinosaur Dawn

Mega-extinction #3: Both land and marine life affected. Reasons: Not well understood. Sea level and climate changes involved.

Mega-extinction #1: 80–90% of Earth life dies. Reasons: Drastic sea level changes; lots of volcanoes in future China.

213

250

286

Jurassic	Triassic	Permian	
	Conifers form large tracts of forest on land. The first mammals and dinosaurs appear, but dinosaurs win the competitive battle in the Jurassic.	Cycads and ginkgos appear. Mammal-like reptiles are common on land. Trilobites are one of the victims of the extinction event at the end of the period, the worst in Earth's history.	

MESOZOIC

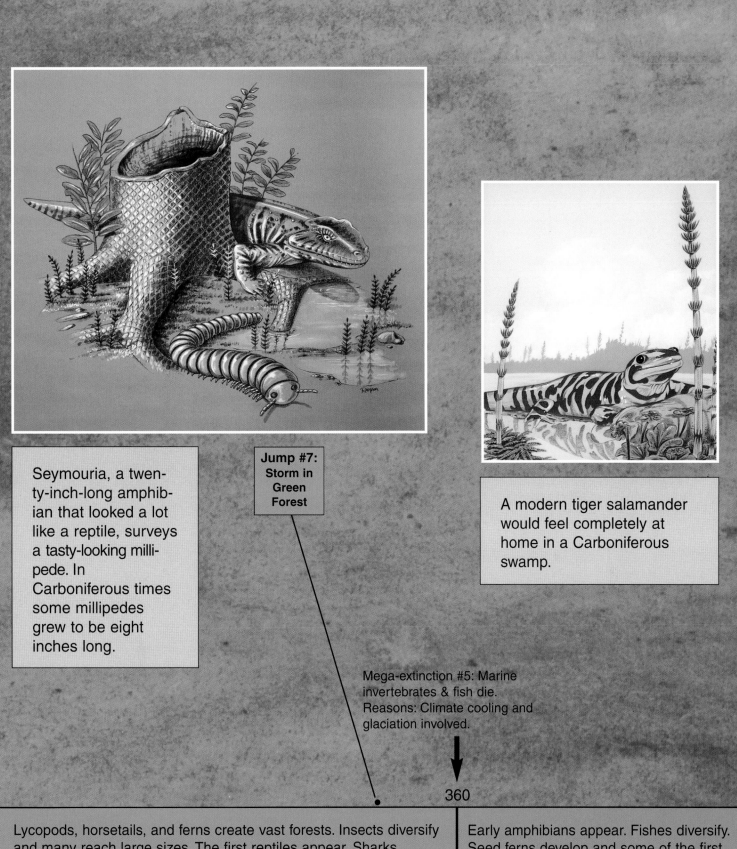

Seymouria, a twenty-inch-long amphibian that looked a lot like a reptile, surveys a tasty-looking millipede. In Carboniferous times some millipedes grew to be eight inches long.

Jump #7: Storm in Green Forest

A modern tiger salamander would feel completely at home in a Carboniferous swamp.

Mega-extinction #5: Marine invertebrates & fish die. Reasons: Climate cooling and glaciation involved.

360

Lycopods, horsetails, and ferns create vast forests. Insects diversify and many reach large sizes. The first reptiles appear. Sharks evolve. Amphibians become plentiful and diverse. Insects develop the foldable wing.

Early amphibians appear. Fishes diversify. Seed ferns develop and some of the first forests appear on land.

Carboniferous

Devonian

PALEOZOIC

Animalocaris, half a yard of tentacled terror as far as trilobites were concerned, was one of the largest predators of its day. It crunched their hard shells with teeth set in a circular mouth.

Jump #8:
Animalocaris
and the
Butterflies
of the Sea

Mega-extinction #4: Brachiopods, trilobites, and reef-builders took heavy losses. Reasons: Climate cooling and glaciation involved.

408

438

505

The first animals and plants invade land habitats. Primitive insects and myriopods develop.

Reef-building animals become important in the oceans. The first fish evolve.

Devonian	Silurian	Ordovician	

PALEOZOIC

Ediacaran animals are named after the Australian location where many of their fossils have been found. They come in various shapes, but all are thought to have had a puffy, "air mattress" look in life.

Single-celled creatures like those shown here have a history dating well back to the Precambrian.

Jump #9:
To What End?

Invertebrate life diversifies in the world's oceans. Trilobites are a dominant animal group that exhibits a new innovation: hard exoskeletons. All the modern animal phyla become established at this time, including the chordates, forerunners of vertebrates.

Cambrian

Beginning of PRECAMBRIAN

The oldest fossils appear about 3.5 billion years ago. The biochemistry of modern organisms becomes established, replacing older, anaerobic microbes. Multicellular organisms evolve.

Transcriber's Closing Comments

The Caretaker must have selected the Olifees' final landing site well, because modern-day Australia has some of the largest outcrops of Precambrian rocks. Most rocks of that age have long ago been destroyed by erosion or recycled into Earth's interior by the motions of its continents. Researchers are, even now, combing the Australian Outback, looking for any clues that might hint at where other time capsules might be or, better yet, where the Olifees might be "sleeping" their way forward through time to their own present.

I hope you've enjoyed this peek into the distant past through the Olifees' eyes. Many more stories are buried in the rocks waiting for someone to uncover them.

Perhaps it will be you.

I could still hear the pterosaurs' sad-seeming cries long after we'd left the lagoon behind.
—Neesha

Glossary
Neesha's Selected Guide to Big Words

A

absolute dating. Any way to figure out the exact age of a fossil or artifact. Scientists like to count the decay products of some unstable atoms (see **radiometric dating**) for really old stuff and count tree rings (see **dendrochronology**) for stuff only a few thousand years old.

abysm. A gulf or really deep canyon. If you're not a poet, you'd probably say "abyss" *(see below).*

abyss. A bottomless gulf or anything profound and impossible to completely understand. For example: Jon's brain is an abyss.

Achelosaurus. A frilled, horned dinosaur (a ceratopsian) found in Montana and first described in 1995. It had two frill spikes but no nose horn.

Acrocanthosaurus. A meat-eating dinosaur (a theropod) in the same family as *Allosaurus (see below)* that lived in North America during the early Cretaceous period. It had a neat, muscular ridge along its back.

Allosaurus. A meat-eating dinosaur (a theropod) that lived in North America during the Jurassic period. Allosaurs stood fourteen to fifteen feet tall and stretched thirty to forty feet in length. Don't mess with 'em.

alloy. A mixture of two or more materials—usually metals.

amber. The hardened (mineralized) sap (call it resin, if you want to sound smart) of pine trees, usually pale yellow or reddish brown in color.

amphibian. A four-legged animal with a backbone that lives part of its life in water, breathing with gills, and part of its life on land, breathing with the help of lungs. You know—frogs, salamanders, and so forth.

Andrews, Roy Chapman (1884–1960). A scientist/explorer with the American Museum of Natural History who went to the Gobi Desert in the 1930s looking for ancient people—he found dinos instead.

Animalocaris. An extinct sea animal of the Cambrian period with segmented claws, a circular mouth with teeth, and no backbone—but it *did* have an attitude, especially for something a foot and a half long.

ankylosaur. An armor-plated, four-legged, plant-eating dinosaur (an ornithischian) that lived from the middle Jurassic to the late Cretaceous periods. Ankylosaurs had clubs on the ends of their tails. Nodosaurs looked similar, but didn't have the club.

Apatosaurus (formerly known as **Brontosaurus**). A large plant-eater with a long neck and tail that lived in North America during the late Jurassic period. One of them could teeter-totter with five modern-day elephants.

argon-40. An isotope of colorless, odorless, gaseous element that doesn't react with other chemicals. (Maybe it should be called a nerdement.)

artifact. Anything human-made or artificially made.

ashfall. A thick layer of ash blown out of a volcano.

asteroid. An itsy-bitsy planet—what Jon would call a planetoid. Most asteroids in our solar system orbit between Mars and Jupiter, but many zip around in other orbits.

Astrodome. A sports arena in Texas.

atlatl. A stick with a notch to hold a spear. It's a fancy name for a spear-throwing thing that lets you stay farther away from animals with lots of claws and teeth.

atomic clock. A "clock" which measures the passage of time by measuring the speed at which various chemical elements decay from one form to another by emitting subatomic particles.

Avaceratops. A frilled, horned dinosaur (a ceratopsian) with a nose horn and two brow horns. First found in 1986.

B

bacteria. Microscopic, living cells and small cell colonies with none of the complex, doubled-layered structures of larger, more common plant and animal cells. Some bacteria do good things for us (like make vitamin K in our large intestines), while others make us sick. Lots of bacteria recycle dead stuff and waste.

balloon vine. The common name for a vine plant called *Cardiospermum halacacabum.* There's a mouthful.

barrier islands. Islands along a coast that partially protect the coastline from ocean storms and waves. Pretty lagoons often form between the islands and the coastal shore. Build a condo there, though, and some giant storm will eventually mash it.

Bird, Roland (1899–1978). An assistant to the famous paleontologist Barnum Brown in the 1930s. He drew very careful and complete maps of dino bones at Howe Quarry in the Bighorn Mountains of Wyoming.

black hole. An old collapsed star so mushed that even light can't escape its strong gravity. That's why it looks black. Duh.

Borg. A *Star Trek* alien cyborg—half humanoid, half machine.

Brachiosaurus. A Jurassic-age, plant-eating dino seventy to eighty feet long and weighing fifty tons. Its front legs were longer than its back legs, and its nostrils flared out of a mound above the eyes.

Brachyceratops. A frilled, horned dinosaur (a ceratopsian). The first ones found were young, and paleontologists didn't know what they would have grown up to be!

Brontosaurus. See Apatosaurus.

bug-bot. An insect-sized robot made by the Tenori. We found out later they also made nanobots (microscopic-sized robots).

C

Camarasaurus. A common, plant-eating dinosaur (a sauropod) that lived in North America during the late Jurassic period. It had a short, bulldoggish face and spoon-shaped teeth.

Cambrian. The period of time in the Paleozoic Era from 510 million years ago to 570 million years ago.

Camelops. A large, llama-like camel that lived in North America during the Pleistocene epoch. Paleo-Indians probably hunted them. They died out 10,000 years ago.

Camptosaurus. A four- to fifteen-foot-long dinosaur (an ornithischian) that probably walked a lot on its hind legs. Lots of these guys lived in Wyoming. Some have been found in Europe.

carbon-14. A slightly heavy, radioactive version of carbon used for dating things (usually used for dating stuff less than 40,000 years old). It has a half-life of about 5,730 years.

Carboniferous. The geologic period from 363 to 290 million years ago. The earliest half is called the Mississippian and the second half the Pennsylvanian. Take a wild guess in what two states they find a bunch of fossils from this time.

carbonized. A critter gets carbonized after it dies when it gets mushed, squeezed, and cooked so much that nothing is left but a thin carbon stain on the rock. Kind of like Mom's toast.

Carnegie, Andrew (1835–1919). A guy who made a lot of money making steel. He thought rich people should spend their money on museums, schools, and so forth, so that's what he did. He liked big dinos.

cast. A form you get when a liquid hardens after you pour it into a mold. (Now you've got to look up **mold,** right?)

caustic. Something is caustic if it burns or eats up flesh. Strong acids are caustic.

Cedrelospermum. An Eocene-age plant that lived near Fossil Lake in Wyoming. You find their fossils in the Green River Formation.

Cenozoic. The most recent geologic era. It started 65 million years ago, after the dinos died. Sometimes called the Age of Mammals.

Centrosaurus. A rhino-like dino (a ceratopsian) with one nose horn at the center of its face.

ceratopsian. Any one of the horned dinos that lived during the Cretaceous period. Most had neck frills and toothless beaks.

chalcedony. A kind of quartz that looks like frozen milk marked with dark spots and stripes.

chlorophyll. A green plant pigment that catches sunlight and helps carbon dioxide and water molecules split, rearrange, and combine to make sugars.

Chronos. Our time-traveling ship! In Greek it means "time."

Coelocanth. A primitive, lobe-finned fish that everybody thought was extinct until some live ones were found in the 20th century.

Coelophysis. An eight- to ten-foot-long dino (a theropod) from the Triassic period. It weighed about fifty pounds and could move quick!

Cope, Edward Drinker (1840–1897). A 19th-century fossil hunter who explored lots of places in the American West. He got into a competitive feud with Othniel Marsh in trying to find the biggest and best dinosaurs.

coral. A hard calcium secretion produced by colonies of marine animals. They form huge wall-like structures called reefs.

crayfish. Looks like a small lobster, but lives in fresh water. It has big claws, lots of jointed legs, and a hard shell.

Cretaceous. The geologic period from 144 to 65 million years ago. This is when **T. rex,** the horned dinos, and hadrosaurs lived.

crinoid. A starfish relative that looks like a stalked plant. They are often called sea lilies or sea stars.

crustacean. A shelled arthropod, usually with claws. Its head and upper body (thorax) are one piece. Crabs, lobsters, shrimp, and crayfish are all crustaceans.

Cybister. A genus of diving beetle still alive today that sometimes got stuck in California tar pits.

cycad. A gymnosperm plant that looks a lot like a palm tree or a pineapple on steroids.

D

Deep Time. A term first used by a writer named John McPhee in 1981 to describe a point in time so long ago (or so far in the future) that it's hard to imagine—just like the term "Deep Space" describes a place so far away that it's hard to imagine.

Deinonychus. A long-armed, meat-eating dino—with wicked toe claws—that lived during the late Cretaceous period. First found in the Gobi Desert.

dendrochronology. A way to figure out the age of trees (and how long ago people lived, if the trees were used for building and so forth) by counting tree rings and studying their patterns.

Desmatosuchus. A Triassic-age, plant-eating reptile with lots of armor plating and spikes on its back.

Diatryma. A giant, Eocene-age predatory bird that had its pick of the pantry after dinos checked out.

dicynodont. A mammal-like reptile that had its day mostly during the Permian period, although some dicynodonts (like **Placerias**) stuck around into the Triassic period.

dike. For geologists a dike is molten rock that seeps into cracks of older rocks. For other people a dike can be a ditch or dirt wall.

Dinomischus. A stalked, filter-feeding sea animal from the early Cambrian period that looked a little like an unopened daisy.

dinosaurs. A group of land-living reptiles that grew to huge sizes. Unlike other reptiles, many dinosaurs walked on their hind legs or with their legs directly underneath them (rather than on the sides of their bodies). Their hips and spines were different too.

Diplodocus. A ninety-foot-long dinosaur (a sauropod) that weighed twenty-six tons and had a dinky head. *Diplodocus* lived during the Jurassic period.

Diplomystus. A herring-like freshwater fish that lived in Wyoming during the Eocene epoch.

DNA. Deoxyribonucleic acid: the sugar-phosphate, double-coil chain molecule that carries the genetic code for living things in the pattern of chemical bases that hold the chains together like a twisted ladder.

Douglass, Earl (1862–1931). A fossil hunter who worked for the Carnegie Museum for many years at what is now Dinosaur National Monument in Colorado. He discovered *Diplodocus* and other neat dinos.

dragonfly. A primitive insect of the order Odonata that looks a little like an old-fashioned bi-wing plane with two giant eyes.

E

Ediacarans. Soft-bodied critters that lived in the oceans starting about 600 million years ago. They looked a little like jellyfish made in a quilt factory.

Edmontosaurus. A plant-eating dinosaur (a type of hadrosaur) first found as a "mummy fossil" in Wyoming.

Einiosaurus. A horned dino (a ceratopsian) that lived in Montana 72 million years ago.

Einstein, Albert (1879–1955). A brainy physicist/mathematician who figured out that mass and energy are just two sides of the same coin. (You know, $E = mc^2$.)

elater. A pointed, elongated plant cell that soaks up water, expands, and helps push spores out of the pod (sporangium) it's in.

Eocene. The geologic epoch from 57 to 34 million years ago.

Equisetum. The Latin name for horsetail plants. They have long, ribbed, jointed stems with a dark pod (sporangium) on the end.

erosion. The wearing away of soil and rocks by water and wind.

eurypterid. Also called sea scorpions, these guys lived in the ocean from the Ordovician to the Permian periods. They're related to horseshoe crabs and look like segmented teardrops with a couple of big, paddle-like legs.

extremophile. Any critter (usually microscopic) that lives where we don't like to be. Bacteria that live deep in the earth or in hot springs, volcanoes, deep ocean vents, and other such places are extremophiles.

F

fabrosaur. A dino that lived during the late Triassic and early Jurassic periods. They probably developed into the ornithischian dinos (the ones that look more like *Triceratops* than like birds).

fault. Don't know, never had one. (Just kidding.) In geology, a fault is a break between layers of rock along which they can "slip 'n' slide."

fission. The splitting of atoms.

fix-bot. One of the friendly little robots on our shuttle that did repairs.

fossil. The mineralized remains of living things and the stuff made by them—like tracks and poop.

Fossil Lake. An Eocene-age lake in extreme western Wyoming.

G

geology. The study of the earth and the rocks and minerals that it's made from.

Ghost Ranch. A ranch in New Mexico where *Coelophysis* fossils were found.

gills. Feather-like structures animals use for breathing underwater.

global warming. Warming of the earth caused by gases like carbon dioxide, which act like greenhouse glass and keep heat from leaking off into space.

Gobi Desert. A crescent-shaped desert in central Asia about 1,000 miles long and 300 to 600 miles wide. Good spot for finding dino fossils.

Goliath. A Philistine giant whom David killed with his trusty sling shot in the 11th century B.C.

grinding stone. A stone used to grind up grain. Sometimes it's called a metate (say: "me-tah-tay").

H

hackberry. A tree of small to large size with toothed, arrowhead-like leaves.

hadrosaur. Also called duck-billed dinosaurs, hadrosaurs were the most common and varied plant-eating dinos of the Cretaceous period. They could walk on all four legs, but could rear back on large hind legs to get at high vegetation.

half-life. The time it takes half of a radioactive element to decay into something else.

hogback. A mountain ridge with fairly steep cliffs on one side and a gentle slope on the other. It forms because the rock layers are tilted about 45 degrees and weather more on the cliff side than on the back side. Looks like a hog's bumpy back, I guess.

Holocene. The last 10,000 years of Earth's history, which is about as long as humans have known how to farm.

hologram. A 3-D image made by photographing an object with a laser beam.

horseshoe crab. A large, shelled, marine invertebrate related to spiders, scorpions, and trilobites.

horsetail. See Equisetum.

hydrogen sulfide. A gas made from hydrogen and sulphur that smells like rotten eggs. Poisonous!

hyena. A doglike meat-eater found in Asia and Africa. They hunt in packs and often scavenge carcasses.

Hyolithes. An extinct, shelled sea critter with a long, conical shell, a fanlike covering (operculum) at the fat end of the shell, and two curved, antenna-like arms that arced back from the operculum.

I

Icarosaurus. A lizard able to glide from tree to tree using membranes stretched over its elongated rib bones. First found in Triassic-age New Jersey.

ice age. A period in Earth history when ice accumulates at the poles and moves into the planet's middle latitudes in the form of huge glaciers. Humans evolved during the last series of ice ages.

igneous rock. Rock that has been heated to a liquid and recrystallized. Feldspar, granite, and basalt are igneous rocks.

index fossil. A common fossil that is typically limited to a narrow stretch of time. That way, wherever in the world you find one, you know the rock it's in is the same age.

Indiana Jones. A fictional movie adventurer patterned after Roy Chapman Andrews.

isotope. A variation of an element with a different number of neutrons (and thus a different atomic weight).

J

jasper. A usually brick-red or brownish red version of the mineral chert, a form of silicon. It polishes up pretty.

Jurassic. The geologic period from 208 to 144 million years ago (the middle period of the Mesozoic era).

L

Lakes, Arthur (1844–1917). A school teacher, writer, artist, and ordained minister who found some of the earliest dinosaur fossils near Morrison, Colorado, in 1877.

Laosaurus. A birdlike dino from the Jurassic-age sediments near Como Bluff, Wyoming. No more than ten feet long.

Lepidodendron. A lycopod tree from the late Paleozoic era that could grow a hundred feet tall or more. Its trunk has a neat, diamond-shaped pattern.

logarithm. The exponent or power, x, to which some number called a base, b, must be raised to arrive at some other number, n. Got that? For example, say you have a base number of 10 ($b = 10$), and you want to know how many times to multiply that number by itself to get the number 100 ($n = 100$). The equation you need to solve is: $b^x = n$, or $10^x = 100$. Because $10 \times 10 = 100$, or $10^2 = 100$, $x = 2$. Thus the logarithm of 100, to the base 10, is 2. A natural logarithm has a base (called e) of 2.71828… .

lycopod. A primitive plant with a stem, roots, leaves, and a spore-holding strobilus at the end of the stem. Modern-day lycopods, like club moss, are small and grow close to the ground. Some extinct ones were trees (see *Lepidodendron*).

M

MacDonnell Ranges. Mountain ranges in the south-central portion of Australia's Northern Territory. From the air the mountains look like marble-cake backbones!

Macginitiea. A relative of the modern-day sycamore tree with fan-shaped leaves.

Machairodus. A Miocene/Pliocene-age saber-toothed cat.

Madagascar hissing cockroach. A large cockroach from Madagascar. The males hiss, wouldn't you know?

mammoth. A hairy elephant from the last ice age. They had big tusks that curved down and then up, and the tusks sometimes crossed. Their molars looked a little like squashed accordions.

Marsh, Othniel (1831–1899). A 19th-century paleontologist who headed the Yale Museum of Natural History. He and Edward Cope competed to find the biggest and best dinos.

mastodon. A hairy, ice-age elephant with gently curved tusks. They had teeth with separate roots and blunt crests.

Meek, Joseph. A "mountain man"/explorer of the early 1800s.

mega-extinction. Usually called a mass extinction. This is when a large percentage of organisms in many different groups die out all over the world.

Mesozoic. The "middle era" of Earth history from 65 million years ago to 225 million years ago. Dinos were top dog, so to speak. The Mesozoic is divided into the Cretaceous, Jurassic, and Triassic periods.

microorganism. An animal or plant so small you need a microscope to see it.

millipede. A wormlike arthropod with a hard, segmented body. Each body segment has two pairs of legs. Veggie-eater.

Miocene. A division of the Cenozoic Era from 5 million to 23 million years ago. Grasslands spread over a fairly dry world.

Mississippian. The earliest half of the Carboniferous period from 323 to 363 million years ago.

mold. A type of fungus that helps rot dead stuff. Their spores come in different colors, which makes them look like fuzzy carpets of green or pink or white.

monkey puzzle tree. A kind of primitive evergreen native to the Andes mountain system in South America.

Monoclonius. The first horned dinosaur ever discovered, found by Edward Cope in 1876. It had one horn on its nose.

Morrison Formation. A reddish, Jurassic-age layer of rocks with lots of dino fossils in it. It's named after an outcrop near Morrison, Colorado.

moss. A simple plant without true roots, stems, or leaves. Moss plants look like soft, green carpets in the forest and make their spores in capsules on tall stalks.

mummy. A dead, very dried out animal or person.

N

Neanderthal. A type of primitive people that lived in Europe, northern Africa, and western Asia during the Pleistocene Ice Age. Neanderthals had heavy brow ridges and stocky bodies.

nimravid. A variety of saber-toothed cat that lived during the Holocene epoch.

Norfolk pine. A primitive evergreen native to Norfolk Island, located between New Caledonia and New Zealand. It is a pretty close relative of the monkey puzzle tree.

O

Ordovician. The period of time in the Paleozoic Era from 439 to 510 million years ago.

ornithischian. A group of dinosaurs that all have birdlike hip bones. Ankylosaurs, stegosaurs, and ceratopsians are all ornithischians. The weird thing is birds evolved from saursichian (lizard-hipped) dinosaurs. Go figure.

ornithomimosaur. A meat-eating, Cretaceous-age dino with long legs, a long neck, and a small head. Lived mostly in Eurasia and North America. If you saw 'em today you'd probably blink and say, "Ostrich?"

ornithopod. The general term for a three-toed dino that ran on two legs (like an ornithomimosaur). The name means "bird-foot."

P

Pachyrhinosaurus. A large, horned dinosaur without a horn! At least, if it did have a horn it was made of keratin (not bone)—like the horn of a modern-day rhino. But it did have a big, bony snout.

Page, George C. (1901–). A wealthy, self-made businessman who gave lots of money to charity. He especially wanted to build a fossil museum for the children of Los Angeles—and so he did.

paleontologist. A scientist who studies past life on Earth by examining fossil remains.

Paleozoic. The era of geologic time from 550 to 250 million years ago.

palm tree. A tall, tropical, flowering tree with feathery or fanlike leaves.

Parasaurolophus. A plant-eating dinosaur (a type of hadrosaur) with a long, knobbed head crest. They made honking noises by blowing air through their head crests.

pelycosaur. A mammal-like reptile that lived mostly during the Carboniferous and Permian periods. Some (but not all) had sail-like fins on their backs.

Pennsylvanian. The most recent part of the Carboniferous period, from 323 to 290 million years ago.

Permian. The period of time in the Paleozoic Era from 225 to 290 million years ago.

photosynthesis. The process in which green plants take sunlight, carbon dioxide, and water and make sugars and oxygen. Neat trick!

phytosaur. A crocodile-like reptile that lived during the Triassic period and probably before. They ate the big, ugly fish that were around then—and probably whatever else got in their way.

Pig Latin. A "language" spoken by taking off the first letter or letters of a word and adding them plus "ay" to the end of the word (like "ixnay" for "nix," or "amscray" for "scram"), so it sounds kind of like Latin. Or you can just drop the first letter and add "lay" to end—whatever you like. Omprendelay?

pill bug. A land crustacean with ten legs that rolls up into a ball when you mess with it. You might call them roly-polys.

Placerias. A mammal-like reptile that lived in Triassic-age Arizona. It looked like an ox with a fleshy mustache.

Pleistocene. The last two million years of Earth's history, during which time there have been a bunch of "Ice Ages." Humans evolved while the ice came and went a few times.

Pliocene. A division of the Cenozoic Era from 2 million to 5 million years ago. Great apes evolved.

polymer. A large molecule (natural or artificial) made up of a string of simpler chemical subunits.

Postosuchus. A very large meat-eating reptile of the Triassic period. Kind of the *T. rex* of their day.

potassium-40. An unstable (radioactive) isotope of potassium that decays into argon-40.

Precambrian. All the time from the birth of Earth to the start of the Cambrian period—4 billion years or so.

Presbyornis. A shorebird that lived during the Holocene epoch after the dinos died off.

priapulid worm. A kind of marine worm about three inches long with a warty body and a retractable snout. Yeah, I hope their mother loves 'em.

prosauropod. Among the first of the veggie-eating dinos. They show up during the Triassic period, and were only *(only?!)* six to forty feet long.

pterosaur. A flying reptile that lived from the Triassic to the Cretaceous periods. Early ones had long tails (rhamphorhyncoids) and later ones had short tails and big heads (pterodactyloids).

R

radiometric dating. A way to figure out the age of rocks by measuring the proportions of radioactive isotopes found in them.

raptor. A bird of prey, like an eagle or a falcon. They term "raptor" is also sometimes used as an abbreviation for "velociraptor"—a dinosaur of prey with big toe claws.

Raymond, Percy Edward (1879–1952). An American paleontologist at Harvard who studied trilobites, red beds, and sedimentation. He is best known for his book *Prehistoric Life*, published in 1947.

red beds. Sandstones and shales that are reddish in color because of iron compounds in them.

relative dating. A way to figure out which of two fossils is older than the other by seeing which one is buried deeper. Not as easy as it sounds, because sometimes rock layers get twisted and folded.

respiration. The process of taking in oxygen to burn up food and produce carbon dioxide, water, and energy (for fossil hunting, of course).

S

salamander. A long-tailed amphibian, usually four to six inches long and sometimes brightly colored.

sauropod. A veggie-eating, lizard-hipped, long-necked dino, like *Apatosaurus* and *Brachiosaurus.*

scorpion. A poisonous spider relative with a pair of claws, four pairs of walking legs, and a coiled tail with a stinger on the end.

sea lily. A starfish relative with feathery tentacles and a long stalk. It looks a little like a flower wearing a suit of armor.

sedimentary rock. Rock formed from sediments *(see below)* after they dry out and get squashed for a long time.

sediments. Suspended minerals and bits and pieces of dead animals and so forth that settle on the bottom of lakes, oceans, and rivers.

singularity. A place where all the dimensions of space and time close up to nothing.

sinkhole. A place where limestone has dissolved away, forming a soil-covered depression or hole that sometimes fills with water.

Smilodectes. A 50-million-year-old species of lemur-like primate from the western United States.

solar cell. A device that collects sunlight and changes it into chemical energy.

sonic gun. A gun that emits high-intensity sound. Makes animals quite uncomfortable.

spore. A usually one-celled structure of primitive plants that can grow into a new plant. Microscopic critters can make spores too.

stegosaur. An armored, Jurassic-age dino with a double row of bony plates along its backbone and a spiked tail.

Sternberg, Charles (1850–1943). A 19th-century paleontologist who hunted fossils all his life in the American West. He worked with Edward Cope in Montana. Charles's sons became fossil hunters too.

strobilus. A conelike structure on plants that produces spores.

stromatolite. A fossil mound made by huge colonies of algae that grew in layers. Today, living stromatolites can be found in salty, protected spots, like Shark Bay, Australia.

Styracosaurus. The horniest of the horned dinos, with a giant nose horn and six big frill spikes. Males probably used the horns to bluff other males and impress females. (Figures.)

supernova. A star that collapses and then blows off its outer layers in one big explosion.

superposition, law of. A geologist's way of saying that in a pile of sedimentary rocks the oldest stuff is at the bottom.

suspended animation. A way of slowing down body functions so you can survive long space or time trips.

T

taphonomy. The study of how a living thing got to be a fossil—kind of a very late coroner's report!

tar pit. A natural ooze of asphalt that forms sticky pools.

Teratorn. A large, extinct meat-eating bird of the last ice age that had a ten-foot wingspan. It hung out near tar pits looking for stuck food.

theropod. A meat-eating dino that walked on its hind legs. O. C. Marsh made up the name, which means "beast-foot."

Thylacosmilus. A Miocene/Pliocene-age marsupial saber-toothed cat-like mammal that lived in South America. Its saber teeth grew bigger and longer than the teeth of true cats.

trace fossil. Something made by a living thing—like a footprint, poop, and so forth—that gets fossilized.

Triassic. The geologic period from 250 to 208 million years ago.

Triceratops. A three-horned, frilled dino from the Cretaceous period.

trilobite. The first shelled arthropod. It had a three-lobed, segmented body with lots of legs and spines and compound eyes.

Troödon. A meat-eating dino (a theropod) that had the biggest brain-to-body ratio of all the dinosaurs. It may have been the smartest too.

tuber. A short, thick, mostly underground plant stem. A potato is a tuber.

tubercles. Bumps on the surface of dino skin.

T. rex (Tyrannosaurus rex). Everyone's favorite meat-eating dino of the Cretaceous period. It had two wimpy forelegs but a huge head with six-inch teeth.

U

uintathere. A rhino-sized extinct mammal that had three pairs of bony knobs on its skull. Some American kinds had a pair of saber teeth (tusks), but they were veggie-eaters.

uplift. A place where the ground is pushed up from forces deep within the earth.

V

vagary. Wandering thoughts or a whim.

W

walking leg. A leg used for walking. Duh.

whiz-bot. A general-purpose, problem-solving, Tenori robot.

wormhole. A connection between two singularities in space-time (see **singularity**).

Y

Yucatan. A peninsula in northern Mexico where a giant asteroid belted Earth 65 million years ago.